Kelly 'n' Me

Also by Myron Levoy

Alan and Naomi
The Magic Hat of Mortimer Wintergreen
Pictures of Adam
A Shadow Like a Leopard
Three Friends
The Witch of Fourth Street and Other Stories

MYRON LEVOY

Kelly 'n' Me

A Charlotte Zolotow Book
An Imprint of Harper Collins*Publishers*

 For information address HarperCollins Children's Books, a division of HarperCollins Publishers,
10 East 53rd Street, New York, NY 10022.
Typography by Joyce Hopkins
1 2 3 4 5 6 7 8 9 10
First Edition

Library of Congress Cataloging-in-Publication Data
Levoy, Myron.
Kelly 'n' me / Myron Levoy.
p. cm.
"A Charlotte Zolotow book."
Summary: Fifteen-year-old Anthony falls for Kelly, the mysterious girl whom he meets singing in Central Park and joins to perform street music all over New York, but their romance is threatened by their very different backgrounds.
ISBN 0-06-020838-4. — ISBN 0-06-020839-2 (lib. bdg.)
[1. New York (N.Y.)—Fiction. 2. Street music and musicians—Fiction.] I. Title. II. Title: Kelly and me.
PZ7.L5825Ke 1992 91-35807
[Fic]—dc20 CIP
AC

For Debbie,
whose music moves through this book

1

I FIRST MET KELLY IN CENTRAL PARK on one of those New York August days when a can of soda is worth more than gold. I was playing my guitar and singing, trying to ease a little money from the endless stream of tourists. I'd set up near the zoo, so I sang happy songs, animal songs, like "Octopus's Garden" or my own "Creepy Beasts." If I ever start a group, we could have a worse name than The Creepy Beasts.

I was really pounding it out and singing like crazy, though my voice is not so great. Add Springsteen and Dylan, then divide by six and multiply by the Cookie Monster, and you've got it. So I was singing, with maybe ten or twelve people watching, my guitar case open for coins, when this girl started singing up the path, five or six benches away. Only six benches away!

It was like being on top of me! What's worse, she had one tremendous voice. A sort of slightly nasalized Joni Mitchell sound, very clear and pure. And loud. Perfect for the country-rock song she was doing. I noticed some heads in my crowd turning.

What a gigantic nerve! Incredible! I took a fast look her way. She was short, not much over five feet. She had this long straight hair—folksinger's hair—and a face I liked, wide-eyed and bright; my kind of face. But I was not in a face-admiring mood just then. How dare she invade my turf! There are unwritten codes! You do not play within earshot of another performer. Never! Ever! This may be New York in August, and heat can drive the natives mad, but you do not ever invade.

I had come early for this great spot. It was along the path that leads to the kiddie zoo with all the farm animals and to the newly reopened regular zoo. It was my spot! But there she was, singing "Ramblin' Man," the good old Allman Brothers song. She couldn't have been more than fourteen. I'm fifteen, and five feet ten and a half, so it would have been no trick at all to stroll up to her bench and lean over and, maybe, spit out a few choice words like *Beat it, sister!* through the side of my mouth, like Humphrey Bogart in those late-night movies my mother watches. I might even have given her guitar a shove or two. Except . . .

Except I really am not into violence of any sort, no matter how mild. Or confrontation. Or anger. Inside,

I can be a pot of boiling oil. But I will not confront. Maybe I've seen too much of that with my parents. I'd sooner change my own spot along the path than start something. I was almost afraid—not of the girl, but rather of what I might do if I let go and lost my temper. So all I did was start singing louder to drown her out.

It didn't work. She could not be drowned. Her soprano was cutting my baritone to ribbons. Her voice sliced through the summer heat like a cool laser beam. And three or four of my people were walking over to her bench.

But her guitar work was not good. Not that mine is Eddie Van Halen, exactly. Still, I could have run rings around her, guitar-wise, if her hundred-decibel voice hadn't been shredding my act. Okay. Good. Fine. No confrontation. I decided I'd start playing *her* song myself. If you can't beat 'em, join 'em, right? So I stopped and tuned to her guitar as best I could, then started banging out "Ramblin' Man" country style, leading in with my buzz-saw voice. And yes, she looked my way, and nodded as if she were taking me on board. She moved a few steps closer to me, nodded again, and we were off and running.

She loved it, I could tell. She edged closer and closer, bringing her crowd with her, and kept looking at me while she bobbed her head back and forth to the beat. We started to play off each other, and I felt united by music and good vibes, as if we were singing in some rally together. Her absolute high was infectious. There was a break in the vocal, and I twanged out a complicated improv guitar solo while she did a little dance in place. We were really together. Then she came in, and I muted my guitar strings and started stomping my foot, because we'd segued into a real country beat now, and she nodded and I blasted off again, and we jammed down that ramblin' highway to a really solid all-together finish. *Karaam!*

Big applause! She blew me a show-biz-like kiss. I saluted back, a real marine-crisp cut. I was covered with sweat, but I felt absolutely great. My anger was completely gone.

As the crowd applauded and whistled, I held my hand out toward her—show biz, again—giving her the credit, which she deserved, while I took a good look at her, close up. She had a red headband on and was wearing torn jeans and wrecked moccasins. Her face seemed delicate—petite, maybe—with these green eyes and light-brown hair that seemed blond in the sun.

In these few minutes, I'd flipped my disc from total negative to something more like I-think-I-am-falling-in-love. There's no telling what can happen in New York in August. . . .

Dollars! We were getting dollars in my guitar case, not just quarters. Three, four. Yes! Five big bucks! We should have started playing again, right away, but neither of us took the lead. So our crowd dispersed, but I didn't care. I was glowing with that perfect spontaneous thing we had done. I wished I could have sealed our "Ramblin' Man" in a plastic block like they do with flowers or leaves. To preserve indefinitely.

The crowd was gone and I became what I usually am when I'm not performing: shy as hell. "That wasn't bad," I mumbled.

"Hey, we were phenomenal!" she said. "Let me get my junk. We've got to talk." She retrieved her guitar cover and a big handbag and dropped them next to my open case.

"I . . . you get three and a half dollars from that," I said, bending down to give her her share.

"No, I only came in at the end of your whole set," she said.

"But I didn't get any dollar bills before."

"Well, okay, just to keep the peace." She pulled one dollar from my case.

"You know, you really shouldn't have set up so close to me," I said nervously. I felt I had to say *something*.

"I know. I guess I was feeling friendly. Your guitar was so good, it was like a magnet. You are something else with that guitar!"

"My guitar is nothing. You—you've got a great voice," I said, still a little shy.

"Want to work together?" She was right in front of me, looking up at my face.

"Just like—just like that?"

"Sure. Why not? Come on! We were great! God, you're so tall!"

I'm only five feet ten and three quarters, to be exact, but if she thought that was tall, why not? "God, you're so short," I bounced back, with incredible brilliance.

"And you're so dark."

"And you're so—so light," I said.

She laughed. "Hey, we could go on like this all day."

"But you are. Are your folks from—like Norway?"

"Me? I'm light 'n' Irish, b'gosh 'n' b'golly. Me mither 'n' father are first generation, direct from the ould sod, they are, 'n' proud of it to be sure. . . . Wait till I tell you my name. Kelly Callahan. How Irish can you get, right? What's yours?"

"Anthony. Anthony Milano."

"Anthony . . ." She paused a minute, as if she were testing it. "Mm. Anthony. I like it. Sort of old-fashioned. And real. So what do I call you? Tony?"

"No!"

"Wow! What's the problem?"

"Nothing. That's what my father called me."

"*Called* you? Is he, you know, like dead?" Her questions kept coming, like balls in batting practice.

"No. Just gone with the wind. He's in California."

"Oh, I'm sorry. . . . God, you are so gorgeous!"

My mind blipped on that. I am definitely not gorgeous. I didn't know what to say.

"No, uh, you're the one who's—who's gorgeous."

"Hey, you're blushing."

"I am not!"

"So Tony-Anthony, you want to try teaming up? We could make a lot more money together."

"I don't know. I might drag you down."

"Come on! Nobody's going to drag me down. I won't let them. I'm the soon-to-become-famous Kelly Callahan. Tomorrow's Whitney Houston. Ta daa!" She held her arms out in a victory pose and looked at me expectantly. "Your turn," she said.

"I'm Anthony Milano, tomorrow's Anthony Milano, and I made about twelve dollars all day, playing pretty good and singing pretty lousy. I am what I am, which isn't much."

"That sounds awful. You gotta have faith! So is it a deal? Callahan and Milano and their trained seal?"

"I don't know," I said. Why was I resisting? Maybe I was afraid of her upstaging me; her voice was so terrific. But I liked her, and it would be a chance to be with her. And she did have faith in herself. I sure as hell needed a transfusion of that.

I took the plunge. "Okay," I said.

"Great! Shake." We shook hands, and I liked the feel of her small hand in mine. She smiled this wonderful smile, an Irish smile, I guess. How could I have resisted for even a moment?

But her smile suddenly disappeared; she was studying something in the distance. I turned and followed her eyes. A girl in a white jumpsuit was walking up the path from the zoo underpass; a girl around my age.

"I've got to split," said Kelly. "Tomorrow morning, okay? Right here? Ten?"

"What's wrong?" I asked.

"Oh, just somebody I don't want to meet right now. Tomorrow? Okay, Anthony?"

"Okay."

As she started walking away, she called back to me, "Of course, I may be out on the West Coast by then. You never know."

"Kelly! Wait a minute!"

"Ciao, ciao, for now!" She was gone. Almost at a run. One song together, and gone. I'd probably never see her again.

The girl in the jumpsuit was at my bench. She was tall and lean; she could have easily been a model. She looked toward Kelly, who was disappearing around a bend in the path. The girl stood there for a moment, then turned to me. "What's she doing here?"

"Do—do you know her?" I asked.

"Oh, do I!" She seemed about to ask a question, then thought better of it. "Look at her run! When you see her, tell her that Michelle, that's me, says she should go straight to hell in a leaky canoe! I mean it!" She turned around and strode back toward the underpass, her body rigid with anger.

I felt a rush of protectiveness for Kelly. But their fight had nothing to do with me. I'd probably never see Kelly again, anyway. She was gone, and I was here. I retuned my guitar and wondered what I should play for my next set. Maybe some good old Simon and Garfunkel. But Kelly's face got in the way. And her *God, you are so gorgeous*. And her eyes. And her hair. And her slight weirdness.

I knew that with the luck I always had, she'd probably go to the West Coast and never show up again. And then her face would become a blurred image, changing and teasing, like a tune you can't quite remember but is always there, always there, right underneath your breath.

It was a little scary, this sudden strange connection. This August mirage.

2

I GOT HOME AT SIX, still thinking about Kelly. I'd decided her face matched her name perfectly. How would that idea work in a song, I wondered.

My mother was out. Good. If she was out, she wasn't in, and that was good, because she hadn't left the apartment for three days. There was a note by the phone in the kitchen:

Anthony—
Am at Krassman's. Maybe something. Don't wait. Take stuff in fridge from yesterday. Back whenever.
Love, Martine.

P.S. Leave my medicine alone!

Translation. Martine is my mother. She's always wanted me to call her Martine instead of Mom, and lately I'd been doing it just to make her happy. More translation: Mom/Martine is an actress; stage, not film. Krassman is her agent. *Maybe something* means she may be getting work. She hasn't had a good offer for over two years, not even summer stock or regional theater. Since Dad split six years ago, Mom's work and income have gone downhill. And since the marriage exploded, she's been drinking, mostly wine, but plenty. That's the medicine she meant; the bottles she stores in her closet. I'm not sure which came first, the wine or the downhill, but they feed off each other, and she's not the Martine Milano she once was. We manage to stay afloat from her TV commercials, miserable ones for discount furniture stores and car dealers in Brooklyn and Queens and New Jersey. We're in our third apartment in five years, each a step down the ladder. Not that we were ever that rich. But at least we had a doorman, once. Now we're on West Ninety-fifth Street, with no doorman, and an elevator that works only half the time. I don't care, but Mom does.

She knows that in the sad real world when an actor's clothes and apartment start fading, it's a message that adds to the downhill look. And downhill begets downhill begets wine and long nights with the TV set, half watching and half boozily asleep.

In our latest downhill event, Mom/Martine is fighting to keep me in private school. The Bennett

School would give her a break, but she cannot admit to the-powers-that-be that she can't afford my tuition. So I've been doing my guitar thing, to sort of help out. I don't think she knows it, but I've slipped some of my money in to help pay for everything from the groceries to new sneakers. If it wasn't for that, I'd probably never have gotten up the nerve to play in front of people. I might have been a closet musician all my life, which might not have been such a bad thing.

I had a sudden curveball thought: What if one thing led to another and I wanted to ask Kelly over sometime and she saw Mom boozy? Oh, God! And our apartment! It was a pigsty. . . . I had to clean the place. It was crazy; I might never see Kelly again, yet I had to clean the place. Now!

I walked around the kitchen. The sink was full of plates with dried eggs and petrified spaghetti. There were cups with dark coffee rims on the table and counter, pans with shriveled vegetables on the stove, and in the refrigerator, a milk container that smelled like overripe cheese. I'd been avoiding it, I admit, waiting for Mom to cleanse the barn, so to speak. I plunged in up to my elbows in pots and pans and lemon-scented dishwashing soap. I even washed the linoleum with wet paper towels and a plastic scouring pad for the caked grease.

It became hypnotic, this cleaning. I hit the bathroom next. I felt sick when I discovered some dried vomit on the floor behind the toilet—from one of

Mom's bad nights, I guess. But I shut my brain off and went to it, using reams of soapy paper towels to sponge it up. I cleaned the tub, which had long strands of hair all over, and then did the sink, which was covered with dried soap goop, like candle drippings.

Then I started working on the living room. Empty wine bottles everywhere; sauvignon, Chablis, chardonnay, Pinot blanc. Clothes scattered all over, and *TV Guides* three weeks old. And soda bottles, cigarettes, used tissues in clumps. And everywhere flowers falling to pieces, their petals all over the rug like a pink-and-blue blizzard—actually kind of pretty and very sad—and photos, photos, photos all over the place. Big glossies of Martine Milano in comedies like *The Last Laugh* and *The Cautious Heart*, and revivals like *Strange Interlude* and *The Crucible*, and even some Shakespeare. I've seen Mom in most of these plays; with Mom an actress and Dad a director, I was a real theater kid before I was five.

I can remember sitting on Dad's lap, in the last row, watching Mom/Martine crying and laughing and saying all the lines she'd memorized in the kitchen, up there on the stage, so made up and young and completely beautiful that Dad would whisper to me, "Is that really your mother?" Dad. Salvatore Milano, the Lady Killer! There were no glossy photos of him, anywhere.

I found a picture under the sofa of Mom as Cleopatra in Shakespeare's *Antony and Cleopatra*, and it really got to me because I was Anthony, too. Mom still shouts a line from the play when I bug her: *O my oblivion is a very Antony!* I studied the photo of Mom as Cleopatra with an asp in her hand. I'll never forget her dying every night, holding that snake to her breast. I was only eight at the time, but I still remember her lines: *Come, thou mortal wretch, with thy sharp teeth this knot intrinsicate of life untie at once*. Or was it *at once untie*? I still don't know what *intrinsicate* really means. I think old William S. meant *intrinsic* but got lost in Toledo. And then the great line: *Peace, peace! Dost thou not see my baby at my breast, that sucks the nurse asleep?* I didn't get that either, but Mom explained. The snake is the baby that "sucks" Cleopatra, the nurse, to death with its poison. Mom always died beautifully. Until the curtain calls, that is. The snake, I'm happy to say, was a stage prop, and I used it to scare the living daylights out of some kids in my third-grade class who kept picking on me because I was such a nerd.

Enough of show biz with Mom. I carefully sorted the pictures and put them in her folders with the clippings and programs and telegrams and pressed flowers. Five folders and seven albums of Mom when she was Martine the Magnificent. That's the worst part of being an actor in the theater instead of in the movies. You have nothing to show after, only yellowing newspaper clippings and phony-looking publicity shots. At least my music, such as it is, is on tape. But I'm never going to act, even though Mom's been pushing me for years. I don't want my future to include lining up wine bottles beside my bed, one after another, at the age of forty-three. Besides, my friend Jason acts. He comes from a theater family, too, and he's already so terrific on stage, I don't want to compete.

I started cleaning my room next. I threw all my dirty clothes into the duffel bag, ready for the Laundromat, put my tapes back into the tape cabinet and my records onto my homemade shelf, then rearranged my posters on the wall. The posters were all freebies from a record store I worked in last spring. I moved Jimi Hendrix next to U2, then next to the Eurythmics, and noticed that Kelly looked a little like Annie Lennox. I moved everything again and put up my Springsteen poster. Then I started combing my hair, trying to find the precisely right casual arrangement over my forehead. A real jock jerk. All I needed was a biker jacket. *God, you are so gorgeous.*

As I rearranged my posters for the third time, I heard the door latches click. It was Mom/Martine. I said the fastest prayer in the world for her. *Let her have something! Let it be good!*

"Anthony."

"Yo!"

"I'm home."

"Yo! Yo!"

"What's going on here? Anthony?"

I could see from my bedroom door that she was dressed in her best summer outfit. "Surprise!" I shouted.

She looked stunned as she examined our newly sanitized kitchen. "It must have taken you hours!" she said. "It's beautiful! The place looks like a *place*!"

"Wait until you see the living room. Come on, Mom—uh, Martine, take a look."

"My heart may not stand the shock," she said. Mom strode from the kitchen to the living room with a grand flourish, pushing her hair back. Her dramatic flourishes were a good sign; she was acting the way she thought an actress ought to act. You'd have to know my mother to know what I mean.

"There it is!" I said. "Clean toenails and all."

"Oh!" she said, staring at the room.

"Do you like it?"

"It's revoltingly clean! Anthony, it is lovely. You've even put all those poor dead flowers in a bowl. I love dying flowers; they're so sad and evocative."

Sad and evocative. Act I, Scene 3, *The Last Laugh.* I picked up the next line, which I knew from some forty performances I'd seen years ago. "They bring back fragile memories for a fleeting moment. . . ." I could not help smiling.

"What! Where have I heard that before?" Mom asked, as if she didn't know.

"Guess."

"*Hamlet*?"

"Not quite."

"*Oedipus Rex*?"

"One more try."

"*The Adventures of Mickey Mouse*?"

"Well, what happened at Krassman's?" I asked, too anxious to play games with her. It had to be good.

"All right. Sit down, Anthony." Great! She only sits me down for good news. She spits bad news out the moment she opens the front door.

"So?" I asked, crazy with impatience.

"So I have a part! It's mine!"

"Where? What? Who?"

"It was Johnny Barnett who wanted me. One of my favorite directors. Strindberg. *The Stronger.* He remembered how I did it, was it five—no, six—years ago? Well, they needed a replacement fast, and I'm it. A little theater in the West Village."

"Great! That's great!" It was a weird short play, maybe twenty minutes long, with two women onstage, but one of them never speaks. I remembered Mom in it. She was terrific.

"Let us not cheer. It's a very modest production. *Miss Julie* is the main event."

Miss Julie was a longer play, also by Strindberg. "I still think it's great!" I said, and meant it. It is not an easy part; she's speaking every moment, and has to go through emotions from A to Z.

"Ah, my Anthony, sweet Anthony, what would I do without you? My only real pal in the world. O happy horse, to bear the weight of Antony!" Another of Mom's quotes.

"Oh, come on, Mo—Martine . . . By the way, which part do you have?"

"Don't worry, Anthony. I'm the talker. Now where's

my Strindberg? It's a big blue book; did you see it when you sterilized the room?"

"No."

"Because I have to get it all set by next Tuesday, and I don't have the script. A rehearsal at nine tomorrow morning. Brutal. But tonight we shall celebrate! Chinese! Did you eat yet? No? Good! Tomorrow you can finish that garbage in the fridge. But right now, we are going to have a night on the town! After the moo shu pork, we may even allow ourselves some Häagen-Dazs."

The dinner was great, with Mom back among the living for a change. She was so up, she was almost manic.

But later that night, when I was in my room fooling around with my guitar, trying to start a song about Kelly, Mom's manic state ended. I could have predicted it. Through my open door, I could see her in the living room, slumped in the armchair, a glass of red wine in her hand. Not again!

I pulled my nails along a guitar string, making it screech like a cat.

I slipped quietly into the living room. The bottle beside her was half empty. "Why are you doing that?" I asked. "You have to work tomorrow, right?"

"It's just medicinal. One must steady one's nerves." I noticed the Strindberg *Collected Works* open on the table beside her.

"You shouldn't do that!"

"I'm fine."

"You said you'd never drink if you had a part to prepare—"

"It's only wine, Anthony! And I'm scared!" She looked beat. No acting now; it was real.

"Scared of what?"

"I read through the play. I can't do it anymore. It's—it's too demanding!"

"Do what you always tell *me* to do! Make believe you're someone else. Right? Someone who will get that part if you don't do it. So you make believe you're that other person. And you do what they would do, and, presto, you're doing it instead of them. Right? Right?"

"Right . . . okay . . . okay. . . . You're absolutely right. A child shall lead you. Anthony, my protector. Watch. I am putting my glass down on the table. See. I am standing up. And I'm going to bed. I'm going to be a good girl. Satisfied?"

I hated the way she made herself the baby and me the parent. But it was better than nothing. Every time I've pushed her to get real help, she goes completely emotional. It's a dead end.

"Okay," I said. "Good night."

"Good night, sweet prince. My Anthony of the musical fingers. And flights of musical angels sing thee to thy rest. And so on, and so forth, *ad infinitum*."

"Good night. You'll be great, just like always. You . . . you gotta have faith." Thank you, Kelly.

"It sounds wonderful, even though you know it's a load of crap. But . . . it's nice to have you on my team, Anthony."

"No problem."

"I wish—I wish I could have given you everything you deserve, Anthony. I wish . . . You know all the things I wish."

"I know. No problem."

3

TEN A.M. CENTRAL PARK. My golden spot just north of the zoo. A beautiful morning. Mom had left for her first rehearsal on time, and sober. All was calm in the August world. The vendors farther down the path were out with their giant balloons, Central Park T-shirts, nameplate bracelets, and plastic dinosaurs. Everything was in place. Even the squirrels were happy. But no Kelly Callahan.

I tuned up and squinted in the sun and started playing. Some early Bob Dylan, a couple of Springsteens, then, just for the fun of it, "I Am a Rock." But business was slow. My crowd consisted of a Japanese family, clearly tourists; three nine-year-olds—two girls and a boy—having fun squealing at every song as if they were at a rock concert; and an elderly couple I see often. That couple must live near the zoo. At the end of my set, after my usual big bow, I got a quarter from the couple, two quarters from the Japanese family, and a couple of dimes, with more squeals, from the kids. They seemed to want to hang around after the others left, and I didn't mind. You need a few people to seed a new crowd.

"Can we make a request?" asked the taller girl.

"Sure," I said, trying to be Mr. Cool.

"Okay. How about 'Lovesexy'?" she said. All three broke out with a round of super giggling. "Lovesexy" has some pretty raunchy lyrics, to say the least.

"I don't know the words," said the wise old guitarist. "Do you?" More giggling.

But wait! There was Kelly, Kelly, Kelly, coming down the path with her guitar strapped to her back, and her red headband, and her ripped jeans. I waved to her.

"Come on. *Pleeez!* Play it," the tall girl said in a mock-pleading voice.

"I can't. There are ladies present." Meaning them. Still more hilarity.

Then the boy held up a dollar. "We'll give you this if you play it."

"Make it ten."

"Okay." Oh, good grief! The boy pulled a ten-dollar bill from his back pocket. Where do they get that kind of money to waste?

"No!" I said fast, to slam the door on it, though I was very tempted. After all, they'd probably heard that song a thousand times. But I am a blusher, and I do not do songs like that before young or old. It's not my kind of music. That's why Prince is a millionaire, while I'm convinced I'll be a flop even before I've begun.

"Hey, Anthony!" Kelly called as she strode toward me. "What's going down?"

"Hey, Kelly!" I called back.

"Anthoneee!" one of the girls sang out. "Lover boy! It's make-out time!" Beautiful! Kelly could hear every word.

She gave me a high five, then unstrapped her guitar and put it on the bench. "Hey, man, I see you've got a group of groupies."

"Lover boy!" all three kids called at once. I would have given them an Anthony Milano sneer, but, well, they were kind of cute in their own obnoxious way. Nine-year-olds trying to be fifteen.

Then Kelly stood on tiptoe and gave me a nice solid kiss on my cheek. "Good morning, Anthony, sweets," she said. She winked at our audience of three, playing to their fantasies. A serious mistake. But I liked the kiss.

"Whoo!" called the shorter girl. "Hot!" Another round of giggles. All three stared expectantly.

"Good-by, children," I said. They did not move.

Kelly tried to resume a normal mode, realizing, maybe, that she shouldn't have encouraged them. She spoke softly so the kids couldn't hear. "That girl, yesterday, when I split, remember? Did she badmouth me?"

"She just said—I don't know why—you should go to hell."

"Oh, she would. That's Michelle. Did she say anything else?"

"No."

"We used to be friends. Good friends. But . . . it's, like, a long story."

"Anthoneee!" our crowd of midget followers called again. Sometimes, I really hate my name. Kids teased me the same way in elementary school. I decided to talk to Kelly as if the three kids didn't exist. Best way. Ignore them.

"So what are we doing?" I asked her. "Want to try to rehearse enough stuff for a set?"

"We don't have to rehearse. We were great just like that."

"Gotta rehearse. We were just lucky."

"Kiss her back, *Anthoneee*!"

"I guess we'd better take a walk, right?"said Kelly. "It's my fault. Sorry."

"No problem. We'll circle around and come back."

"Lover lips! Kiss her back!"

We walked up the path with the gleesome threesome right behind us. *Anthoneee! Kissy kiss!* Nothing we did could shake them off. We went out of the park. They followed. We thought of taking a bus, but I hated to waste the money I'd just made. So we walked up Fifth Avenue, on the park side, the Terrible Three right behind us.

We passed some derelicts sprawled out on benches

by the high stone wall of the park. Kelly, without breaking her stride, dropped a dollar bill in each man's lap; one, two, three. It made me feel kind of selfish and stingy, not wanting to even take a bus. But I knew Mom needed all the extra help she could get. Still, Kelly certainly was generous. I liked her all the more for it.

One of our kid followers called toward us, "Give *us* some money! A hundred dollars and we'll leave you alone!"

I suggested we get some doughnuts and coffee over on Lexington Avenue, to get rid of them. They followed us right into the coffee shop. We turned and went right out; they turned and followed. They were like pit bulls; they would not let go.

They started a singsong chant, "We want Anthony! We want Anthony! Kiss, kiss kiss!"

Okay! Enough! I do not confront, but this was too much! "You kids beat it," I ranted, "or I'll punch you out!" Brave Anthony Milano, the scourge of Manhattan.

I hate to admit it, but the kids just laughed. I took a threatening step toward them, but they danced back. They loved it.

"I mean it!" I shouted. They laughed again. I took another step toward them.

"Wait, Anthony," Kelly said, grabbing my arm. "I've got a better idea. My mother works in this building on Fifth Avenue and Seventy-eighth. She's a nanny. Let's go there. No way they can follow us up."

"A nanny? You mean, like, for babies?" I asked, still staring as angrily as I could at our three musketeers.

"Right, except Andrew's seven years old. See, she takes care of Andrew. But the whole family went to England for a month, and she had to go with them. Their apartment's empty. The maid's the only one there. Caitlin. But I think she's off today. Anyway, I've got a spare key. So let's go."

We headed up Lexington Avenue, with our groupies right behind us. "Anthony! Wait for us!" The chorus began once more.

"So you mean your mother is in England?" I asked, trying to have a normal conversation over their noise.

"She sure is. It's just me and my dad, right now. We could go to my place, but it's way over on Ninety-fourth and First. Too far. Besides, I don't want you to see it; my dad's the janitor there and we live in this basement apartment. It's awful."

"You should see my place," I said.

We turned on Seventy-eighth Street and headed back toward Fifth Avenue. Kelly stopped abruptly in the middle of the block, in front of an iron gate that led to an alleyway behind the huge apartment buildings that fronted on Fifth Avenue. Our three monsters stopped a short distance behind us, but their chorus continued.

"*Anthonee!* Lover lips!"

"Okay," said Kelly. "Here's where we shake the kids. This leads to the service entrance. I've got the key to the gate, because I used to visit my mother during the day. It's okay; they let me. Ready? Let's go!"

She unlocked the gate quickly, and we both slipped through. Then she closed the gate with a bang, before our three musketeers could follow. Kelly turned and blew them a kiss.

They pressed against the gate. "No! We want Anthony! *Pleez!* Anthony, we love you!"

I waved to them as I followed Kelly through the alley behind the high buildings. One of the girls chanted after us, "You're going to make out! You're going to make out!" All three picked it up. "YOU'RE GOING TO MAKE OU-UT! YOU'RE GOING TO MAKE OU-UT!" We raced to the back entrance of one of the buildings. Some fast maneuvers with another key and we were in. The service elevator was right there.

"This is it," said Kelly. "Let's go up. Come on, don't worry. It's okay. Honest."

She pumped the button and the elevator door slid open. This service elevator was a lot nicer than the regular one-and-only elevator in my own apartment house. It was light tan, and had a fan that went on automatically. Kelly pressed the button for the fourteenth floor.

I felt a little weird, like an intruder in someone else's life. Kelly just leaned against the wall and shut her eyes. At the fourteenth floor, the door slid open and we were in a tiny vestibule. The rear door to the apartment seemed to be the only door there. Did this mean there was only one apartment for the entire fourteenth floor?

Kelly jiggled another key, shook the door a little, turned the knob, and we were in. It didn't seem that incredible. There was a small foyer and a couple of ordinary rooms. Plain and simple. No big deal. Except that these were only the servants' rooms.

"See?" Kelly pointed. "That's my mother's room when she sleeps over, which is pretty often. It's her home away from home. Want a look?"

"Well, maybe just from the door," I said, feeling like a total intruder. One thing I noticed immediately: Her mother's room was extremely neat, unlike the bedroom of a certain mom I will not mention.

"Okay, folks," said Kelly as if she were giving me a tour. "That's one of Mom's hats over there; she wears hats all the time. She's kind of old-fashioned. And over there, that's a picture of her with Andrew. The kid she takes care of? Nice kid, Andrew, though he can be a real brat sometimes. And there's my grandparents back in Ireland. And over there's a picture of me when I was a little kid. See? I'm wearing a dopey ballet outfit. So what do you think? Can you tell what my Mom's like from the picture?"

"She seems nice. She looks very warm and all," I said, studying the photo. Her mother was quite heavy, and she had this wonderful, round, open face. She looked ready to step out of the picture and hug you.

"She *is* warm. She's terrific. I really love her to

pieces. There's one of her and my dad. Isn't he handsome?"

"Uh-huh," I murmured. He was very tall compared to her mother, with darker hair. He looked a little stern, as if he thought taking photos was a foolish waste of time.

We walked down the corridor and turned right. I gasped. The room we'd entered was enormous, like a huge loft. It was light and airy with super-modern furniture of glass and stainless steel. There were giant cushions on the floor in groups of three or four, and a beautiful beige rug with brown-and-orange designs woven in, and a long dining table made of crisscrossed steel and thick glass. On one wall, I saw figures of a man and woman made entirely out of bent neon tubes. Kelly pressed a button, and everything lit up; they became a blue man and red woman taking turns pointing at each other, on, off, on, off, on, off. There was a huge stone fireplace with a painting on the left by Picasso, no less, and on the right, another painting that Kelly said was by Franz Kline. The Kline painting had these enormous black strokes against a white background; it looked like a giant Chinese character, the kind made with an ink brush.

As I walked slowly around the room, I saw paintings and little statues everywhere. It was like being in a gallery at the Museum of Modern Art. I was afraid to touch anything. There were three floor-to-ceiling windows at the far wall, with beige drapes that matched the rug. I noticed, to my surprise, some low trees and bushes right outside the windows. As I looked more closely, I realized that there was a big terrace and garden just outside. This had to be a multimillionaire's apartment.

"Want to go outside?" Kelly asked. "We can."

"Oh, uh, no thanks." I did, but I didn't want to show that I did.

Kelly put her guitar down on the long glass dining table. I hesitated, then decided I'd better not.

"Put your guitar down, Anthony!" she said. "Throw it on the table. You're acting as if this is a cathedral, or something. It's just another garbage dump done up in glass and stainless steel, that's all. Do you know what? My mother told me they have roaches! Just like the rest of us! So stop acting so—so in awe."

"Well, you're used to this. I'm not. I've never seen stuff like this except in a museum. Some of it's pretty weird. Like that painting over there? It looks like a blown-up comic strip."

"That one's by Lichtenstein. They described all this stuff to me once. They gave the slum kid the grand tour, right? There's one by Georgia O'Keeffe. And that one's by a guy named Clemente. Let's see; all those little statues with the holes in them are by Moore. Disgusting, right?"

"Why? They're great. What's so wrong with owning art?"

"It's that they're so spoiled, the Lawrences. They don't appreciate anything they have. Including my mother, and believe me, they *have* her. They pay my mother shit. They really do. And they're so prejudiced. My mother says she heard them, behind her back, call her a mick donkey, just because she made a little mistake about something or other with Andrew. That's the Lawrences. Andrew got a suit he outgrew in four months. Three hundred and fifty bucks. You know how many homeless people could have dinner for that?"

"Well, maybe they give a lot to charity."

"Sure, if it makes them look good, so they can get on the big-deal committees. That's what my mother says, anyway. Hey, I've got a great idea. Maybe we could steal something and sell it, and use the money for really poor people. Want to try?"

"Steal?" What was I getting into?

"Sure. Like one of those little Henry Moore statues. They wouldn't even miss one; they have so many. They're big on Moore, because she's British, like the artist. That's why they visit England a lot; her parents still live in Manchester. Plain working people, my mother says. But you wouldn't know it from Mrs. Lawrence's fancy accent. You know, she worked in his Wall Street firm; that's how she met him. Robert Lawr—"

"I don't care!"

"No, listen. Now she's trying to be part of the power crowd, even though he couldn't care less. But he does what she wants, and—"

"I don't care about the Lawrences!"

"So what do you care about?"

"I care about you."

"Okay. What do you want to know?"

"I want to know why you would steal something."

"Because I hate them."

"You'd get caught! And it's wrong! How can you give money away to street people one minute, then start stealing the next?"

"*The Adventures of Robin Hood* fell off the top shelf and hit me on the head when I was a kid."

"I'm serious!"

"You always are. Come on, Anthony! You really believe me, don't you?"

"You mean you were kidding?"

"Yes!"

"Oh . . ."

"Hey, I know what. Let's make those kids happy. Let's make out. Right on the rug under that Picasso. We can dedicate it to the Lawrences. Much better than robbing them." I couldn't tell if she was kidding again. But she seemed to have this other side to her, a tough cool way of talking that troubled me.

"Just like that?" I said.

"Sure."

"You want to make out with me, just to spite some people you don't like? Thanks a lot. Do you do this sort of thing all the time?"

She started shaking her head, as if I were a hopeless case. "God, Anthony. I don't believe you! You're smarter than that! Can't you tell when someone's putting you on? Get on my wavelength! Please!"

“Well, maybe I can’t! Maybe I’m not as smart as you think!”

“Oh, yes you are! You keep putting yourself down! You do! Like: ‘I’m Anthony Milano, and I’m going to be Anthony Milano.’ You can be anything! That’s what I’m going to do! I’m going to be what I want! Who I want! Not like I used to be.”

“Okay . . . I guess I’ve got to get used to you. I guess I believe what I hear.”

“I know. But if you do that with me, you’ll go crazy . . . Anthony Milano. I’m not used to a guy like you, either. My friends always wisecracked and put each other on. I guess it’s a habit with me by now. I’m sorry. I am. Sweet Tony-Anthony.”

“I’m not sweet.”

“Oh, yes you are.”

“Kelly, could we get out of here? This place really spooks me.”

“Me, too. Oh, does it!”

“But first . . .” I led her over to the Picasso painting next to the fireplace. Then, in my own sensationally clumsy way, I kissed her. It was a warm, warm kiss, as if we’d been kissing for years. “There,” I said. “Right under the Picasso. That was for you *and* the Lawrences.”

She put her arms around my shoulders. “One more. For me, only,” she said. So we connected, again, a still warmer kiss.

I was liking this a lot, but I was also getting pretty nervous. I’d never done all that much with a girl before. Yes, I was as naive as hell. But she pushed me away. Very gently, very nicely, but she pushed me away. Believe it or not, at that moment I was almost relieved.

"No more, sweet Tony-Anthony," she said. "We two have to become acquainted, like my mother would say. . . . Let's do some music in the park."

She took my hand and led me out to the foyer and the elevator. I stopped and turned her around for one last kiss. After the kiss, we stood there for a long time, just hugging. She was so small, I felt like a blanket around her.

"Let's go," she finally said. "Anthony . . . I've already got a guy. He's in San Francisco. I'm sorry."

Bang! It was like when a guitar string snaps and the music goes suddenly sour. My luck, as always.

4

WE SAT ON A HILL OVERLOOKING the sailboat pond, humming and strumming our way through a dozen songs, new and old, trying to get our act together. The boats—white, blue, yellow—kept rearranging with every breeze, like those colored glass chips in a kaleidoscope. Once, long ago, my father and I had sailed a boat there. My sixth birthday.

I'd decided to bury my feelings about Kelly and her San Francisco boyfriend. She had a right to have boyfriends anywhere she liked. I would be businesslike. Music was a business, the same as any other. She was my business partner. And we were doing a rehearsal. Period. The end.

It took us ten minutes just to get in tune with each other. My guitar is not the best; its high E-string keeps loosening up on me at the worst possible times, and I have to retune after every song. Kelly could tell my guitar was an *el cheapo* special. She borrowed it to try a few notes, then made a face.

"I'm getting an awful sound," she said. "It buzzes. I don't know how you make it sound so great."

"It's all in the little finger of the left hand."

"Anthony, where did you get this thing? It's like a little kid's guitar." She looked inside the sound hole to check the label. But there's nothing there; the guitar is anonymous.

"It *is* a little kid's guitar," I said. "My father gave it to me when I was nine."

"Oh. So you've been playing a long time. No wonder you're so good. . . . Say, how old are you anyway?"

"Me? Fifteen. Why?"

"Hey, you're just a kid! I'm sixteen. I'm old enough to be your mother!"

"You can't be sixteen! You look maybe fourteen at the most. Are you putting me on again?"

"It's okay; everybody thinks I'm younger. I need some zits, then I'll look my age. So are we going to try that last song again? Maybe we should start with that funky bass line you made up."

"Sixteen!"

"Come on, Anthony! Who cares! You're hung up on age. It doesn't make any difference."

She was right. It shouldn't matter. It *didn't* matter. Anyway, we were just business partners. She could have been thirty-five. Business is business.

She plucked a few more notes on my guitar, then gave it back. I asked if I could try hers; I'd been eyeing it all day. It was a Guild acoustic, really nice.

"My guitar likes you," she said as she handed it to me. "See? It's wagging its tail." Another big smile. I love her face when she smiles.

"How did you get a guitar like this?" I asked.

"I saved for over two years."

Her guitar had a good rich tone; I could feel it in my body. I can always tell a good guitar. I've tried them all in those music stores down on Forty-eighth Street, where the guitars and banjos and bass fiddles hang overhead like ripe fruit. Endless guitars. I love to go down there and try them out, the really expensive ones: the Martins, aging and mellowing like fine wines, and the Gibsons from the sixties and early seventies. Talk about richness of tone! Of course, I can't try them too often or they'll recognize me and throw me out.

We went through a few more songs, and it was a whole new thing with her guitar. A double thumbs-up. Right then and there, I promised myself I would save for a good guitar, too. Mom would have to get less of my take. She had work now, anyway, so money would be coming in.

When I did my second solo break, Kelly started going *Hey, great man! Yeah!* We sang louder, then louder still. We were really getting into it; the rehearsal was turning into a performance. People looked our way. It felt great. It always felt great, playing with Kelly. We ended the song with a slow fade-out. Nice.

"You were *fabuloso*," said Kelly.

"It's your guitar that did it."

"Then let's switch. You take my guitar and I'll take yours."

"No!"

"Go on. Keep it."

"No way! Someday I'm going to get a really good one. But they cost a thousand or more."

"But we want to be as good as possible right now! So go ahead and use mine. In fact—I don't know how to say this—maybe you should mostly play, and I should mostly sing. What do you think?"

It was a nice way of saying that my singing was awful. Well, she was right. I'd been thinking that for a long time. "I've got a better idea," I said, trying to ease the sting. "Let's trade voices."

"Oh, you'd really sound lovely. We'd get a crowd for sure. . . . You look like I shot an arrow into you. Did I?"

"Yes."

"Come on! We have to use our strong points, right? That's what's good about a team. It doesn't make sense for me to play guitar when you're around. . . . Tony-Anthony? Please smile. Pretty please? You're cute when you smile."

So I smiled. And she burst into a bigger smile. I did like this crazy girl, no matter what. She seemed so happy that I wasn't insulted. I moved toward her and gave her a quick kiss, boyfriend in San Francisco or not. She didn't pull away.

We decided to do a set down by the sailboat pond, in front of the statue of Hans Christian Andersen. The best spot around here was at the other statue, the "Alice in Wonderland," but a violinist was playing Viennese waltzes there. He's always there, dressed in a tuxedo; he sort of owns the spot.

As I played and Kelly sang, I could feel her clear voice around me like a silken scarf. We two were alone, together, in the world of our song. The intertwining music was like a kiss, a long, long kiss. This is what making love must be like, I thought, real love, even though I'd never done it.

We ended up doing not one but four sets, getting better and smoother and more coordinated with each number. Kelly's voice and musicality was simply phenomenal. She could tell what I was going to do with the guitar almost before I did it. I loved every moment of our performance, though I was sweating buckets while she remained amazingly cool.

By two P.M. we'd had it; it was becoming another August broiler. But we'd made over thirty dollars in less than two hours. And our competition, the violinist, had the bigger crowd all along to boot. Even splitting it with Kelly, it was more than I'd ever made before, even on a weekend at the zoo.

We sat on a bench in the shade, grazing on hot dogs and ice-cold orange soda, while the Viennese waltzes glided past us, rich as whipped cream.

"Do you know," Kelly said, "we could actually make a living doing this."

"Can you make this much working alone?" I asked, hoping she'd say no.

"Sometimes. But two people are better. With two of us, it's a real show. So are we a team?"

"Yes. Definitely."

"Great. We could meet every day at ten. I'd like to play other places though. I know some dynamite spots. Like over near the Plaza Hotel. Or, where I make the most money is down in the subway stations—"

"You play in the subway? All alone! It isn't safe!"

"Sure it is."

"You could get mugged!"

"You can get mugged anywhere. It's good money. People really like to hear music down there in the tombs. It cheers them up. It's like seeing a flower in a prison, someone said. They just *throw* quarters at you. You'll try it, right?"

"I guess."

"Okay, I've got to go. See you tomorrow at the zoo. Or maybe—hey, Anthony? I know another great spot. It's down at the South Street Seaport. How about, let's meet at the zoo and go downtown to the Seaport. It's nice down there. Ocean breezes. Okay?"

"Okay."

"But now I've really got to split."

"You always have to split. Why?"

"It's, like, well—my father. I have to help around.

Like I told you, he's a janitor. And he's got arthritis and stuff."

"Can I go with you and, maybe, hang out awhile?"

"No. I don't want you to see my place. It's a mess. It's really bad. Do you mind?"

"My place is a double mess, but I don't—"

"Anthony, I don't want you to come with me. I just don't."

"Okay."

"So don't look so angry."

"I'm not angry."

"Yes, you are. . . . Anthony, there's this guy in San Francisco, like I said."

"So?"

"So you shouldn't be thinking about me the way you are."

"What way! You don't know what I think!"

"Yes, I do. Why would you want to hang out with me and watch me clean out garbage pails?"

"Well . . . I don't know." She had me.

"I'll be going to San Francisco soon."

"Oh . . ."

"I haven't told my folks. I'm trying to see—like with what we're doing—to see if I can make enough to live on."

"But your parents. Why would you do that to them?"

"Well, my guy's out in San Francisco, right?"

"Right . . ." The *my guy* really, really hurt.

"Hey, I've got to get home now, for sure. My father

will have a fit and a half."

"Kelly? Do you think anybody could ever make you change your mind?"

"Like who?"

"I don't know. . . ."

"Like you?"

"Yeah. . . ."

She looked at me without a word, and I may be crazy, but her eyes were signaling *yes*. I could tell. Was it a galloping case of wishful thinking? No. She was really looking as if she wanted to say *yes*.

"Well?" I finally asked.

"I wish I could explain," she said.

"*Explain!* Tell me! What?"

"I can't. I have to do what I'm doing. I swore to myself I would, and I'm going to, no matter what happens. I've messed up everything else; I don't want to mess this up."

"I don't get it."

"I know. See you tomorrow at ten." And she was on her way out of the park.

Kelly Callahan kept slipping away from me every time I saw her. There was something about her I couldn't catch hold of, something that didn't make sense. It used to be that way with my father; he would be great, then suddenly he became another person. A totally distant person.

When Kelly and I did our music together, I felt so close to her. And when we kissed, I knew she meant it. But then the doors shut, the windows slammed closed, and she was inside her house, and I was outside, alone, as if nothing had happened. It was hopeless. How could I compete with her unseen boyfriend a continent away? He was a ghost. In a way, I felt that Kelly was a ghost, too. What could I do? Nothing.

But wait a minute. Wait. . . . What if, just maybe—what if I wrote a really great song about her? About us. Like John Payne would do in those old-time movies I watch with Mom. A song she couldn't resist. Just Kelly 'n' me, and baby makes three. My song would win her over. Love would conquer.

Some chance.

5

SO I TRIED TO WRITE A SONG. I sat in my room with the door shut and the blinds closed, sat in the dim light and let music flow through my brain. I stared at my long shelf of records, my earthly treasure. Those records have been packed and unpacked so many times in our downhill moves from apartment to apartment that I keep the empty boxes, folded flat, under my bed.

I hummed snatches of my song-to-be, trying to let the collected musical power of all the records fill my head with spiritual vibrations. And I began to hook into an idea.

Some people do lyrics first, some the music, but I do both at once. I played some notes on my guitar and hummed again. Then I sang to myself, moving my head back and forth like Stevie Wonder.

Your face is music,
That can set me free. . . .

Free of what? I liked the first line, though. I picked something out on the guitar, to try to make her face become music. High notes against a bass. Not bad. Not bad. Okay . . .

Your face is music,
Like the sound of the sea,
Like the call of a bird—

Yes! I was on a roll!

In its place, on a branch, in its home . . .
On a windblown tree.
On a windblown tree, oh yes,
On a windblown tree.

Not bad. Wasn't there a windblown tree, though, in some other song?

Your Kelly face is in my mind
Like a tune I love,
Like a song I forgot . . .

Song I forgot. Wait. Song I forgot. Wait. Wait . . . Okay.

That teases and changes and hides
Like birds in a windblown tree.
In a windblown tree, oh yes, oh yes,
In a windblown tree.

And I try to hold it, like mercury,
Like mist, or a memory,
But it's here and it's there,
And it's gone like the call of birds

In a windblown tree, oh yes, oh yes,
In a tree. In a windblown tree.

That's the way songs come to me. Fast, once I get in the right groove. I played the song a few more times and scribbled the words in my notebook. I can't write the music; I just memorize all my chords.

I thought maybe I could play it for Kelly over the phone, right then. And I realized—idiot that I was—that I didn't have her phone number. I could try looking up all the Callahans on East Ninety-fourth Street. Well, why not! It was an idea. I checked the directory. Weird. No Callahans on Ninety-fourth. Not a one.

I figured they might have an unlisted number, so tenants couldn't call and complain at all hours. We had a super once who did that. Well, I would definitely get her number tomorrow, and give her mine. But how I itched to sing her my song.

I played it over and over, changing the melody a little, trying some guitar riffs, fixing a few words here and there. And again and again, I pictured Kelly going outrageously bananas over the song, and, naturally, over me.

Jason called at about five thirty. Jason Wainwright is my best and, maybe, my only real friend. He was his usual overexcited self on the phone. He was having a party this Saturday, and his girlfriend, Nicole, had located a strobe and one of those reflecting globes that revolve overhead. For free.

"So listen up, guy," Jason said. "I want you over by

eight, okay? To help us with everything. Can you get some beer?"

"No."

"Damn. Well, I'll have to get my fake ID revved up. Would you, friend Anthony, mind bringing that ukulele of yours along? And maybe play a little at the height of the orgy? Nicole will give you a kiss."

"Sure," I said. Then, in a flash of Milano brilliance, I thought of Kelly. Yes! Absolutely! I'd ask her! What harm? San Francisco was over two thousand miles away. Yes!

"Hey there, Jason-hasten-get-the-basin, I'm bringing a friend, I think."

"A fwiend! You have a fwiend? What kind of a fwiend? Is it female? Have you decided to go straight?"

Jason's parents are both actors; they were in a play together in Connecticut. They only got home on Mondays which made it pretty easy for Jason to have parties whenever he liked. I met Jason years ago when our mothers both appeared in Chekhov's *The Cherry Orchard*, Off-Broadway. We threw spitballs onto the stage from the wings. Chekhov probably would have approved—a touch of realism—but they barred us both from the theater.

As I said, Jason is a terrific actor. He's been in three Equity plays already and had a small part in a movie they were going to be shooting in New York. The only trouble is, he's almost as mock-dramatic, sometimes, as my mother. Or dramatically mocking. Mom doesn't like him; she thinks he's too theatrical. It takes one to know one.

Some people think Jason is gay, but he isn't. It's just the way he is. Not that it would matter to me. Underneath all the hype, Jason is a very gentle soul, of which there are not many. That's why I like him, even with all his wiseass remarks.

"Tell me more about your fwiend," he said.

"Look, I just met this girl, and I want to bring her if she's free, that's all."

"Oh? But what if she charges?"

"Jason! I'm serious!"

"Well, Anthony, it's high time. You found yourself a nice girl, so good! Settle down, get a steady job, have a few kids, it's a life!"

"Please. No more shtick. I'm serious. I like her. I really do."

"Oh, you *like* her! Good God! Did you say *like*! Be still my heart! Where did you meet this trollop?"

"In the park. She was singing. You ought to hear her voice."

"Oh, good. Bring her voice along with your ukulele. . . . Hey, buddy, I'm happy for you. You've been the most girlfriendless guy I've ever known. . . . She must be weird to like you."

"Yeah. She is."

"Weird is good. Thank God for weirdness. Where would we be without it? Bored out of our socks."

"One other thing. She says she has a boyfriend in San Francisco."

"Oh . . . well, that's okay. I don't mind. But she only gets half as much beer and pretzels at our 'do,' since she's only half with you. Fair is fair, right, big fella?"

"Thanks. I feel much better about it now."

"I knew you would. But look out. She sounds interesting. I may steal her from you."

"Thanks again."

"Just kidding, Milano. Peace, pal. I gotta run. So long, sewer mouth."

"So long, Wainwrong." My little Jason Wainwright farewell. It rhymes, you see.

I must say, that stealing bit got to me. Jason is very good-looking, and quick with his mouth, and can be funny, all unlike me. I'd actually gone out with Nicole first, after I'd met her at a party. Then we went on a double date with Jason, who never stopped talking, mostly to Nicole. He talked; she laughed. He talked some more; she laughed some more. And it was farewell, Nicole.

Maybe he isn't such a gentle soul. Maybe I just want him to be. Maybe I need the ideal friend who doesn't exist, except in songs and daydreams.

I daydream a lot.

6

THERE WAS A COOL BREEZE off the East River, rippling all the pennants on the huge, four-masted ship *Peking* moored at the South Street Seaport. It's always carnival time at the Seaport. There's clowns and jugglers for the kids, open-air beer gardens and restaurants for the adult kids, and endless food stands indoors. I love the place. From an upper deck at the end of the pier, you can see New Jersey and the Statue of Liberty and the big ships moving slowly out into the Atlantic. They've restored all the buildings and surroundings to make you feel as if you're back in the 1800s. And the Fulton Fish Market is right there; it smells to high heaven when you get up close enough to look inside the big, dark, barnlike structure with its long counters for fish. The fish selling ends by early morning;

only the smell remains.

On the subway downtown, I'd asked Kelly for her phone number. She wrote it on half of a pink bus transfer, and I gave her mine on the other half. I'd been right; her number was unlisted. Then I asked her, very casually, if she'd like to go to Jason's party Saturday, and she said *Okay. Why not?* No mention of her San Francisco boyfriend.

We started playing out on the main pier of the Seaport, near the bandstand, where the *Ambrose* lightship is docked. She gave me her guitar, and I gave her mine, as if we'd been doing it all our lives. It reminded me of how Mom and Dad, when they were being silly, used to exchange hats, right out on the street. And all three of us would keep walking as if nothing were wrong. It was a game with them.

We got a nice crowd of kids with their parents right behind, purses and pockets bulging with money, I hoped. We began with a round of "The Drunken Sailor," for a nautical touch. As I went into a solo, Kelly jumped out in front of me and started doing sort of a clog dance or jig. Then I jumped in front of her, while she stepped behind me, and I did a Milano dance, very original, looking like a drunken gooney bird rather than a sailor. The kids loved it. We kept it up, changing places, dancing, singing, faster and faster, while I pounded away at the guitar—Kelly's guitar—trying to keep my fingers on the right frets, and it was, as they say in upper-crusty circles, all rather high-spirited. In other words, it was a blast.

We did more sea chanteys, then one more "Drunken Sailor."

We made eight dollars and thirty-five cents in that one set. Two cops walked right by us and didn't say anything. We weren't sure, but Kelly thought you needed a permit to perform here. But we didn't care. Let them arrest us. The day was great! *We* were great!

In the next set, after another round of sea ballads and jigs, I announced that I was going to do a solo. Kelly looked surprised but nodded and sat down, squatting right on the wooden deck with the little kids, which is what a Kelly like my Kelly would do. And I started to sing:

> Your face is music,
> Like the sound of the sea,
> Like the call of a bird
> In its place, on a branch, in its home
> On a windblown tree.
> On a windblown tree, oh yes,
> On a windblown tree.

When I got to *Your Kelly face is in my mind Like a tune I love . . .* I saw Kelly look down a moment, then up at me. She was biting her lip as if there were some kind of battle going on inside her. She stared right at me for the rest of the song. Big applause. The crowd liked it, particularly the adults.

"Thank you. Thank you," I said. "We'll be taking a short break. Your generosity is famous throughout Manhattan, and we appreciate it."

The adults gave their kids coins to put in Kelly's guitar cover, and some bills, too. I turned to Kelly and smiled, trying to hide how uptight I was over what she thought of the song, and me. She looked very serious.

"Did you write that song for me?" she asked.

"Uh-huh. I did it last night."

"Thank you. It's a terrific song. You really like me that much?"

I nodded, feeling awkward as a potato.

"Come on," she said. "Let's go out to the end of the pier. We've got to talk."

We sat on a bench on the upper deck of the pier, facing the Brooklyn Bridge a quarter of a mile away. You could see the cars endlessly flowing from Manhattan to Brooklyn. The crisscrossed support cables of the bridge always surprise me; they're so intricate and beautiful. I heard somewhere that the two towers of the bridge were once the highest manmade structures in the world. We sat silently for a while, watching gulls and boats go by.

"Okay," Kelly finally began. "Here's the story. There is no boyfriend in San Francisco. I made it up. I'm a liar. Okay?"

"Okay." What would come next? Had she lied to get rid of me?

"See, it's like this: I don't want to really fall for anybody. Not now. I can't. I've got to be on my own. So I gave you this story. Anthony, I thought about you a lot yesterday. I didn't write any songs, but I thought a lot.

About both of us."

"That's great! I think."

"Well, maybe not. I don't know. If I say I like you, then it'll be even harder, right?"

"Why? Why can't you just let things happen? *Do* you like me?"

"Yes."

"You do?"

"Oh, you bumblebee brain! Of course I do! Can't you tell?"

"No. I don't know. Maybe . . ."

"But I *am* going to the West Coast by the end of the summer. I swear I am. So what good is it for us to start something?"

"But why? Why the West Coast?"

"To get away. I have a girl friend out there I can stay with. I've just got to get away. I want to be Kelly Callahan, even it if kills me. And I can't be Kelly Callahan here. I don't like what I am, or I should say *was*. If you knew what sort of person I was, you wouldn't be sitting here. You wouldn't even spit on me."

"Try me."

She looked at me as if deciding whether or not to take the challenge. Then she bit her lip again. She did that whenever she was upset. After a moment, she shook her head slowly.

"No. I'm not staying here, not even with you. Every minute, every second is a new life. That's Zen. I read some books on it. I'm going to act like a new me until

I become a new me. Which I almost am."

"But what's so wrong with being the old you?"

"Never mind."

"Kelly, I like you. I like you a lot. I meant what I wrote in the song. But right now, I could punch you right in the face. You're so—so damn frustrating!"

"I can understand that. Go ahead." She stuck her face out toward me, eyes closed. "Go ahead."

I leaned over and kissed her. I'm obviously as crazy as she obviously is.

"Coward. . . . Hey! Enough of this!" she said. "I'm starving. Do you like Greek food?"

"I never had any."

"It's great. And healthy. We can get some at one of the fast food stands inside. You can eat in ten languages in there," she said, pointing to the building behind us.

I wanted to try just one more time to find out what was going on. "Kelly, listen," I said. "I want you to know you can tell me anything, anytime. Okay? I'll tell *you* something. My mother is an alcoholic. I wouldn't admit that to anyone else, not even my best friend, Jason."

She shrugged. "I'm sorry your mother's got a problem," she said. "But I'm not going to play doctor with you, Anthony: You show me yours and I'll show you mine. If I'm not okay just as I am right now, then walk away. Please. Just walk away."

I sat there while an East River gull hovered nearby, fighting the breeze, rising, falling, rising again, then dipping away and off.

"Okay," I said, not moving.

"Okay," she answered. "Let's eat."

We went inside and bought some spanakopita, which we ate as we walked back down to the main deck of the pier. Our spot had been taken by a magician in a purple outfit. So we walked farther on, to the cobblestoned street, and did three more sets opposite Sweets Restaurant. By three thirty, we had made a total of fifty-two dollars and change. Kelly thought her voice was beginning to go, so we decided to call it a day.

"Hey," said Kelly, "I'm getting hungry again. How about let's walk up to Chinatown and get some noodle dishes. I know a great place."

"How can someone your size eat that much?"

"Easy. I actually weigh a hundred and ninety pounds. I'm small, but I'm dense. In body and brain."

As we strolled toward Chinatown from the Seaport, we passed right under the huge approach ramp to the Brooklyn Bridge. From sunlight into gloom. This was the New York tourists didn't see. It was bad. Nothing but weeds and strewn garbage and abandoned cars with their hoods and trunks sprung open, like busted limbs, and all the windows smashed. Above us was the beautiful bridge with the spiderweb cables, but here below, it was a morgue.

We passed some derelicts lying against a chain-link fence. There were more of them up the block. Not the safest place in the world to be walking. But Kelly started dropping dollar bills in their laps, one after another. She was doing it again. It was the money she'd earned all day! Why did she spend five hours singing in the hot sun for this? I could see giving a few quarters maybe, but not this. She'd given out ten dollars in a few minutes. Without a word. Without these men even asking.

As we came out from under the bridge into the sunlight, I asked her, "Why?" I always seemed to be asking Kelly *why*.

"Oh, that's the new me, too. I've saved enough for plenty of shrimp chow fun, don't worry."

"But what about shrimp chow fun tomorrow?"

"Oh, tomorrow I'll sing again. Simple, right?" And she looked up at me and smiled.

Was she trying to be some kind of saint, or was this just another part of her weirdness? The more I knew her, the more I didn't know her. And the more I wanted to find out.

7

FRAGMENTS OF DEEP RED LIGHT bounced along the walls and slid across the ceiling of Jason's darkened living room. The speakers were delivering Sonic Youth at full blast, and twenty lunatics, including Kelly and me, were swinging their arms and torsos in an attempt to dance—or I should say, move—to the pounding beat. It was Jason party time, with all systems go.

We'd arrived late, but it was no problem. The party had blasted off without us like a berserk spaceship. We could hear the music vibrating in the hallway the moment we got out of the elevator. The door to Jason's apartment was unlocked, so we just pushed and entered. His normally quiet living room was a dark-red bat cave of noise and beer smell. You could feel your body pulsing to the beat. I would have bet that

Jason's parents could hear the roar of the speakers all the way up in Connecticut where, as I said, they were starring in a romantic comedy in a summer theater. The neighbors must have been in Connecticut, too.

Kelly and I and Nicole and Jason screamed our hellos at each other over the blaring music. Not the best way to meet a new friend. Jason screamed about beer and pizza in the kitchen, and screamed for us to raise hell. I screamed back at him, questioning why he needed my guitar—actually, it was Kelly's guitar—with all this racket going on. "Great! Great!" he shouted toward me and Kelly. Then he gave Kelly a sort of hug, and shouted, "Any fiend of Anthony's is a fiend of mine."

Jason likes to pick a theme for his parties, and the theme tonight was clearly punk. I had not been told. Many of the dancers were dressed in leather jackets or complete leather outfits. Studded belts and bracelets and purple hair surrounded us. These were our normally mild pals. I guess it was really something of a costume party, but Kelly didn't know. It looked for real. Maybe it *was* for real. I hadn't seen most of these people lately. Maybe a transformation had taken place. Paul over there, who'd been studying cello for the past six years, was wearing a biker outfit with a pair of handcuffs hanging from his belt. We'd almost become really good friends, Paul and I, but he'd never been able to escape from his endless cello lessons to do anything else. Our eyes met and he gave me an embarrassed shrug as he danced in place.

Good old Paul. I guess he'd had one cello lesson too many.

I felt I'd gotten lost in a low-budget punk-rock movie, where the director had told everyone to improvise. It was crazy! This wasn't us! This was downtown, but we were uptown. We were regular churchgoers, synagogue-goers, or at the extreme, New Agers who went into Central Park at the summer solstice to join hands and hum. In fact, Jason had had a New Age party last year complete with crystals, incense, and assorted gongs and bells.

So this was obviously punk night, but Kelly didn't understand, and it was too unbelievably noisy to explain. She was dancing, but I could see she didn't like it. She looked at me, shook her head, but kept on gamely jumping around to the hammering blast of the music. I shouted toward her, "HEY! DO YOU WANT SOME PIZZA?"

She looked at me as if she were about to barf and shouted back, "GOD, NO, ANTHONY!"

We danced and crashed into people and furniture, and tried to get with it. I made up my movements to match the music, and so did Kelly. In a sweaty, aerobic-exercise way, it was actually fun, except for the decibel level. I know a kid who lost most of his hearing from being so close to blasting speakers. I've brought earplugs to some of Jason's parties, but this time I'd forgotten.

As we danced, I detected the wry sweet smell of pot; it seemed to be coming from one of the bedrooms. I'd tried some once at one of Jason's festive events and ended up coughing for a week. "I HATE THAT SMELL!" Kelly shouted. I was bothered by that. Was she judging the smell or was she judging my friends?

The strobe light came on, fluttering white against the red fragments from the overhead mirror ball. We moved and didn't move, held in suspension by the flickering strobe, as if we were all in an old Keystone Cops movie or a lightning storm. Jason came over with some cans of beer and pushed one into my hand and one into Kelly's.

"HEY, DRINK UP, PARDNERS!" he screamed.

Kelly put the can down on the table, all in strobe-light slow motion, and yelled toward me, "ANTHONY! PLEASE! LET'S DANCE!"

"SURE! SURE!" I shouted back. "NO PROBLEM!"

But no. Jason was back and trying to cut in on me with Kelly. He put his hand around the back of her neck to signal her to turn toward him and dance. He does that to girls sometimes; he means it as a friendly gesture. But Kelly turned and pushed his hand away. "DON'T DO THAT!" she shouted over the music. Jason laughed and tried it again.

As Kelly swung her arm around, it seemed to jump crazily in the strobe light. Her fist, for a flickering second, seemed frozen in flight. I heard a sharp *crack* over the blasting music as her fist caught Jason perfectly on the left side of his jaw. His head jerked sideways; his expression was blank in the sudden jolt. I'll never forget that surprised look, caught like a photo finish in the strobe light. Then he recovered and tried to laugh it off.

"I'M OUT OF HERE!" Kelly shouted to me, heading toward the door. "ANTHONY, PLEASE!" I grabbed the guitar and followed her.

"HEY!" Jason shouted as we left. "I LIKE THAT GIRL! SHE'S GREAT!"

We were in the hallway. My ears were still ringing from the music, and the hall seemed to buzz before my eyes, as if there were a strobe light here, too. Jason had been wrong. But Kelly didn't understand. We walked to the elevator silently. She had punched my friend and walked out of his party. I felt like an idiot.

"I hate guys manhandling me," she said in the elevator. "But—I guess I shouldn't have hit him. I'm sorry."

"No problem. He's just my best friend, that's all."

"Oh. . . . Hey, listen, Anthony. I'll go back and apologize if you want."

"I don't know . . . he grabs girls a lot. Maybe he had it coming."

"He's like some of the guys I used to know. I guess I saw red."

"That's because the lights were all red."

"I'll go back up and apologize. Okay?"

"No. Jason pushes me around, too. Let him stew a little."

"I'm sorry, Anthony. I really messed up your party.

But your friends—that's the kind of crowd I used to go with. Only mine was worse. They're not like you at all, your friends."

"Yes they are. It's all bull. Jason must have told them to wear leather. Only he didn't tell me."

"Do you want to go back? Really, I'll go."

"No. I—I have a better idea. My mother is rehearsing for this play downtown and she's not home—"

"Is your mother an actress?"

"Yes."

"Oh, wow! You never said."

"And so, like, we could go to my place and put some records on, and have a party of our own. A quiet party." The Milano mind works slowly but surely. Maybe the Jason Wainwright punch-out—which I knew I'd hear about for the next month—maybe it was for the best. The thought of being alone with Kelly, dancing close, made me so nervous I had trouble keeping my famous cool. "We could, you know, raid the refrigerator and listen to records and—"

"Maybe we *should* go back to the party."

"Why?"

"I don't want to get involved, Anthony. Like I said."

"I know. Just records. Okay? And turkey salad. Our fridge is full of turkey salad. Okay?"

"Okay."

As we walked up Central Park West and over toward Amsterdam Avenue, my mind raced between Kelly and my apartment. Had I made my bed? I was obsessed! I didn't want Kelly to see my room with my pajamas and dirty underwear lying around. At least I'd rearranged my posters.

Our apartment house is shabby. There's no other word. The front door sticks every time, and the lobby smells vaguely of cooked cabbage. Someone on the first floor must always eat cabbage. The elevator has graffiti scratched into its wood walls, including a new one that announced *Puerto Ricans Get Out!* I'd crossed out a similar message last week, but it had reappeared. As the elevator bumbled upward, I whipped out my pocketknife and scratched the new message into incoherence.

"Good," said Kelly.

"This isn't the greatest building in the world," I said.

"You can see it everywhere. People hating people. Sometimes I think New York's about to explode. You know there's an empty crack vial on the floor there."

I looked down. There was a little plastic tube in one corner. I must be naive, but I couldn't tell if it was a crack vial, even when I saw it. "Are you sure?" I asked.

"Of course!"

That "of course" was so certain that I wondered all over again about what she was keeping from me. Had she been into crack? She could tell me. *That's the kind of crowd I used to go with. Only mine was worse.* Why wouldn't she tell me?

I undid our double lock and ushered Kelly in, hoping and praying that Mom had washed the dishes before going to the theater. "This is it," I said to Kelly as we went into the kitchen. Hooray! The dishes had been done. "Our Rembrandt painting is at the dry cleaner's right now, but we've got a terrific wall calendar over there." I heard the TV set from the living room; Mom must have left it on, as she often does when she leaves in a hurry.

"It's a better kitchen than mine," said Kelly. "If the refrigerator works, and the stove works, and the water runs, you're in good shape in New York. Right?"

"Right. Want a turkey-salad sandwich?"

"Great!"

We slapped together a couple of sandwiches and I poured some milk. A lucky bonus: The milk didn't smell. As we carried our stuff to the living room, I hoped that Mom had left it in half-decent shape, too. Now that she was in rehearsals and feeling more and more up, she'd started paying attention to—

Oh, no! There in front of the TV was the one and only Mom/Martine, sitting in the middle of my life when she was supposed to be at rehearsals! Then I realized that there were no rehearsals on Saturday evening; they had paid performances at seven and ten P.M.—the usual Off-Broadway schedule—and Mom wasn't taking over the part until Tuesday. Still, she should have been there studying how the present actress was doing the role!

She sat there, staring at the TV screen but not really seeing it, her mouth in a familiar depressed sag, her eyes dull. And the old faithful glass of wine was in her hand. Perfect! Just perfect! Well, there was nothing I could do but introduce Kelly.

"Um, Mom, uh, Martine. This is a friend of mine. Kelly Callahan. Kelly. This is my mother."

"Hi!" said Kelly with an upbeat lilt.

My mother turned toward us slowly, as if she were under sedation. I hadn't told her about Kelly. I hadn't had a chance. In these past few days, she'd been so busy that we'd left each other notes on the kitchen table.

"Oh. Kelly?" Mom asked, trying to slip the wine glass out of sight. "Should I know who you are?"

"I'm a friend of Anthony's. I'm sorry. I didn't mean to bust in on you like this."

"Oh, no, no, no, no! Any friend of Anthony's is a friend indeed."

I rushed to explain. "Uh—Kelly and I, we met in the park the other day, and we've been singing together. Sort of a team. And I—we came over for sandwiches because Jason's party was pretty lousy, so we—"

"Ahh! I was just on my way out," Mom said. "Florence and I—you know my friend, Florence, Anthony—we were going to a film. So have your sandwiches and I'll be on my way."

"Mom. It's okay."

"No, I'll be on—"

"Really, Mrs. Milano," said Kelly. "We just stopped by for a second and—"

"Mrs. Milano!" said Mom. "Who in the hell is Mrs.

Milano? The name is Martine. So, Kelly. You sing?"

"You should hear her voice," I said.

"I'm sure it must be quite lovely. But give it up. Give it up, Kelly." How many glasses of wine had Mom had?

"Pardon?" said Kelly, super politely.

"Singing. Give it up. The performing arts are nothing but endless pain. Do I state that clearly? Give up singing. It will eat out your insides. The performing arts are for those who are made of cast iron and rivets and possess an ego as big as the Washington Monument. One is raised up, only to be crushed. Over and over. It's all so hopeless."

Kelly looked at me and nodded slowly. And in that nod I could read her unsaid words: *So that's where your lack of confidence comes from.* Did it show that much?

"What happened today, Martine?" I asked. She was in her usual funk for a rehearsal in trouble. At least she wasn't too wiped out from the wine. This was her verbally depressed stage rather than her silent depressed stage. Verbal was better.

"Nothing happened! That's just it. When you play a monologue against a dunce, nothing *can* happen. But I'm through, Anthony. This is my last appearance on the legitimate stage. I hate to subject you to this, Kelly-the-singer. But there it is. Three more days and I'm on, and it will be a disaster. That turkey salad is probably moldy by now. If you should become ill, do not sue us, Kelly. We will skip town.

Give up your singing and become a realtor. Everyone makes money in Manhattan being a realtor. My hairdresser sells real estate. My doctor does. Even that man who peddles books on the street in front of Zabar's does. Are you two just friends, or are you *friends*?"

"Just friends," I said.

"Ah. Well, any friend of Anthony's—or did I say that? I forgot you had a party at Jason's, Anthony. I forgot. I thought you wanted to see *Top Hat*." She started explaining to Kelly, "You see, Anthony and I watch the old movies together on, um, well—but we've seen this one before, and . . ."

"We could all watch it," said Kelly. "I like the old movies, too."

"Oh, no, no, no. You two—I was going to see a movie with Florence—except I'm watching a movie here. I didn't know—I . . ."

In that moment, with that lost look on Mom's face, I realized suddenly how lonely she must have been, how lonely she was, sitting there thinking I was going to be home any minute to watch *Top Hat* with her. It was the same look she used to have so often after Dad left.

Kelly sat down next to her on the sofa and pointed at the TV screen. "Fred Astaire is still the king and world champion. I could watch this movie a hundred times."

"So could I," said Mom.

I parked myself on the other side of Mom/Martine.

"If I made it," I asked, "would anybody have some popcorn?"

"Me!" said Mom loudly, playing the little girl again. She actually put her hand up.

"Me, too," said Kelly.

I went into the kitchen and got out the popcorn maker, and made a huge batch. And we sat there by the TV, the three of us, eating batch after batch of popcorn, while Fred and Ginger did their thing.

Kelly looked toward me every so often, past Mom sitting between us, and smiled her Kelly smile. She understood. Me, my mother, the whole bit. As my mother would say in her theatrical way, this wasn't a Kelly. This was a *Kelly*!

8

I SAT IN THE BIG PLAYGROUND near Eighty-sixth Street, practicing chords and riffs on my guitar, while waiting for Jason. He had called after midnight and said he wanted to talk to me, and we agreed to meet here Sunday at one P.M. Enough time for him to recover from all that beer and pot and mega music. And that blow to the head.

This playground had been my favorite spot in Central Park when I was little, my meeting place and hangout. Jason and I still meet here a lot; it's a kind of kids' clubhouse to us that I guess we don't want to completely give up. It's some fantastic playground, with this huge twenty-foot-high wooden beam, like a skyscraper girder, that you can walk across or sit on. And lower down, there's a long narrow bridge with chains for railings, and all sorts of posts, platforms, ropes, and slides.

It was a perfect day for doing music in the park, cool for August, and cloudy. But Kelly had to do something today, a mysterious something that involved helping some friends move. Our next big musical event had to wait for Monday afternoon; we were to meet in front of the Plaza Hotel at two thirty P.M. to amaze the unspeakably rich with our act. Maybe it was just as well; I didn't feel like playing serious music today. I needed some time to think.

I plucked the strings of my old beat-up beauty and watched the kids swarm over the high bar and the chain bridge and all the decks of the make-believe fort. A couple of them were almost as old as me, macho guys doing a dance on the girder to a salsa beat from a nearby radio. They both were dressed in nothing but shorts, and I envied their muscles. I've tried working on developing my arms and chest, lifting weights at Jason's place, but nothing seems to happen. That's one reason I don't go to the beach much.

But why did I feel so sad? All these kids shouting and playing and having a good time, and I felt sad. Some of the best times I'd ever had were in this playground. The first time I ever went out with a girl—Joan Carlin, in seventh grade—we'd ended up in this playground. We'd started out with Burger King and a movie, and then strolled over here because we'd suddenly realized we'd both played here a lot when we were younger, and must have seen each other, maybe even fought for the slide or the ropes, but couldn't remember if it ever happened. So we walked over, just to see if we would remember. It was dusk, and the kids were gone. And we kissed—my first real kiss—under one of the tall platforms, leaning against a support post. Joan and I went together for five months, until she moved to Massachusetts. We never did anything more than kiss, but it was enough.

Way before I met Joan, my father would take me here on Sunday afternoons, when he wasn't working on a play. As I've said, he's a director. Pretty famous now, I guess. Salvatore Milano, only he shortened his name to Sal Milan when he went to Hollywood. He used to let me run wild while he read scripts, smoking his endless cigarettes. Once when I was thirteen, and he was long gone, I managed to get a pack of his brand. I wanted to try to smoke one, to try, I guess, to imitate him. But I gagged on the cigarette and had to stop. So I put it in an ashtray and let the smoke fill the room. His smoke. I remember I suddenly started crying. Very crazy. After, I opened all the windows and waved a newspaper around, trying to get rid of the odor. I thought it was all gone, but when Mom came home, the first thing she did was ask me if Dad had been there. She *knew* he'd been there. The amazing thing is she didn't know *how* she knew. Since it's a big scene whenever Dad really shows up, which is almost never, I confessed what I'd done and handed over the cigarettes. She threw them right out the window, but didn't say anything more to me. That night, she got totally bombed.

As I was saying, Dad would sit on a bench and go through seven or eight scripts in gray, blue, or brown covers. But always, at the end of the afternoon, he'd put down the pile of scripts and play with me. Maybe I was seven or eight. I'd hold on to this long knotted rope, and he'd pull it way back, and I'd swing clear across the playground, back and forth, while I gave off my jungle cry. Now, when I see other fathers playing with their kids here, it makes me feel kind of empty.

It was my father who gave me the guitar on my ninth birthday. I loved it. I loved holding it close and feeling the sound vibrating out of the wooden cavity. I loved the power of it, making up my own music. I could change my mood by changing the guitar's mood, from deep moaning chords to the highest shrill pings, like the clink of glass. I would pick out notes and make up bits of songs for hours. I even dreamed of it in my sleep.

A few months after I got the guitar, a kid I knew taunted me about my father having a girlfriend. It was on the way home from school. I told the kid he was a liar and threw a half-full soda can at him. There was this comet of soda, but I missed him completely. When I got home, I asked Mom. She started crying, and I realized it was true. Dad moved out the next week, promising that he'd see me every weekend. A month later, he flew to the West Coast. Now, when he comes back, maybe twice a year, and takes me to dinner and a basketball game—I hate basketball—we have nothing much to talk about. I mean, there's a lot I'd like to say, but I don't know how. He wants me to come out and see the West Coast with him and Norma—that's her name—but I haven't yet, and I think I never will. I'll see it by myself, someday.

Anyway, it's just me and Mom against the world now, or at least that's the way she sees it. But I wish she'd find someone else besides me to be against-the-world with. I'm getting tired of watching old Hollywood movies, and having to be companion, cheerleader, and shrink. I want to be myself, whoever that is. I really understood what Kelly meant when she said she wanted to be Kelly Callahan even if it killed her. Only it might be easier for her; her parents sounded like they were all together, while Mom is so lost so much of the time.

Jason showed up at last, just in the nick of time. I was getting into a Mom-type depression, and I needed to get on a different track fast. Jason looked hung over, but Jason always does, he has such lazy-looking laid-back eyes. Perfect for the film star he probably will become.

"Hey, Milano," he said.

"Hey, Wainwright."

"I see you've brought your ukulele with you. You ought to have that old thing shot and put out of its misery."

"Right. Uh, Kelly wanted me to tell you that she's sorry."

"For what?"

"For belting you in the jaw and wrecking your party."

"Wrecking my party? Man, she *made* the party! It was the event of the evening. What a swing she's got."

"Anyway, she's still sorry."

"And from someone that small. She is kind of short, isn't she? We understand, Milano. You've got to have a girl you can overpower. But look out for her right hook, friend."

"Jason, you really shouldn't be putting your hands all over people. You grabbed her neck. You do that all the time."

"I *touched* her neck. I'm not going to apologize for that. That's me. It's the way I am. Friendly. I like to make human contact."

"Then girls are going to belt you."

"Only dweebsville types. You've got to be a dweeb to think I did something wrong. She didn't go for the beer either. Or the pot."

"Neither did I!"

"We know you're a saint. Saint Anthony of the Milanos. Come on, Anthony. It was a party. People hug each other at parties. Face it. I was right. She was wrong. But being large-hearted, I accept her apology. Now let's never mention it again. It's over and done. By the way, I think she loosened a tooth."

"Good!"

"My lawyer will be in touch."

"So is this why you wanted to see me?" I asked.

"No. Much more serious. Anthony! How would

you like to be in a movie?"

"Okay, I'm supposed to ask what movie. What movie?"

"You know, the one I'm going to be in, in September. *Street Power*. They have a scene out on a pier. I think they're going to use the one off Seventy-second Street, where people sunbathe. And they need a guy playing a guitar. I'm in that scene, too. We'd be together. You'd even have a couple of lines. Nice? I mentioned your name."

"What would they want me for? I'm no actor."

"Oh, who *is*! I admit I dropped a few names, like your mother is Martine Milano, and your father is who he is. So they figure you're like the Barrymores; it's in the blood."

"Well, my answer is no."

"Maybe it's for the best. Because they said they need a good guitarist, a guy who plays really well. And come to think of it, your playing leaves much to be desired. I'm being kind."

"Thanks."

"You'd never get past the audition."

"You may think you're kidding, but you're right. I stink."

"Definitely. Except they've already heard you play, and you've passed."

"What! How?"

"Simple. I gave them my copy of that tape you made. Haw haw."

"Hmm . . . I passed?"

"Yup."

"But they don't even know what I look like."

"I showed them a picture."

"What is this! You're acting like you're my agent or something!"

"I am. I expect fifteen percent. Make that twenty; you're a difficult client. Look, Anthony, I saw this opening, a mile wide. You were perfect. So I plunged. I was going to tell you last night, but you and your boxing companion left in a hurry."

"I don't know . . ." I was weakening. Despite all her gripes to Kelly, I knew Mom would love to see me do some acting, even in a small part.

"They still have to look you over and give you some sort of screen test. But I think you've got it if you want it. Say yes, Anthony! You'll actually get paid."

"Can they use a girl, too?"

"A goil who things thongs, perchance, lover boy?"

"You got it."

"Sorry, buddy-boo, but I think you're supposed to be a loner out on the dock. And I come along and hear you playing and ask you something. Like *Where'd you get that lousy guitar?* So it's just you. Say yes, Anthony, or I'll punch you in the teeth and get even for last night."

"Yes." Why not? It sounded great. Only I hated to leave Kelly out. But she might be in San Francisco by then anyway.

"My man! We are going to be in a moovin pitchur together. It may actually get on TV if they can sell it.

Okay, Milano! Let's celebrate! I'm going to walk the high bar as in days of old. Dare you to follow me, chicken."

We climbed up to the beam from the first post, which has some footholds on it, and I must admit, I was scared. How had I ever done this years ago? It was high! And narrow! They say as you get older, you get more afraid. But Jason stood up, arms out, and strolled across. I took a step or two, and froze. One more step, and I wobbled. Then I backed up three steps, knelt down, and worked my way off, slowly.

Jason had strolled back along the wooden beam and looked down at me. "Hey, Anthony," he called. "What's wrong?"

"I forgot how high it is."

"It's easy, as long as you don't think." He climbed down and joined me. "It's like acting. You're scared, but you do it anyway. Okay, Anthony, for real. I'm sorry I made your friend think I'm a lout. Are you guys okay? You and Kelly?"

"Sure."

"Good. That's what counts, right?"

"Right."

"Hey, you know something?" He stopped and watched the kids going down the slide.

"You were saying?"

"I'm scared, Anthony. Not high-bar scared. The real *it* scared."

"What's the real it?"

"Life. My life out there. That's my high bar. If I

don't make it in acting, I'm wiped out. Splat!"

"That's crazy!"

"I know. I know. But I'm still scared. My folks don't know from failure. You make it, or you're nothing. That's them."

"Who cares what they think? They don't own your life. Or your brain. Jason, you'll be okay, whatever you do. You're the smartest guy I know. It doesn't have to be acting— Are you listening?"

"I always listen to my wise old buddy. Okay! You're right! I have to kick my parents clean out of my head. Take that! And that! . . . There. Got 'em both on the first try. . . . You're right. Only—you know, Anthony? Sometimes I wish I was a little kid again. Like that one going down the slide."

"So do I," I said. "So do I."

9

I WATCHED A WHITE STRETCH LIMO, as long as two normal cars, maneuver daintily into a double-parked position in front of the Plaza Hotel at Fifty-ninth and Fifth Avenue. I was a little early for my two-thirty rendezvous with Kelly, but I didn't mind; I was enjoying the Megabucks Scene beneath the huge iron awning. I don't know if the Scene was enjoying me with my beat-up guitar and worn jeans and torn T-shirt, but that wasn't *my* problem. The white limo stood there for a moment, not doing anything except getting people to stare at it. But you couldn't see in; it had reflecting glass windows. I often wonder what happens behind all those pitch-black windows. I usually picture people making out, but I'm obsessed.

After a while, the chauffeur came around and

opened one of the rear doors, and a man and woman got out. The man had on a gray pinstripe suit; you could have sliced a baked ham with the sharp edge of the trouser cuff. His shoes were so shiny, they seemed to be made of black porcelain. He looked at me with total contempt. For a moment, I understood exactly what Kelly felt about the Lawrences, where her mother worked. I'd like to have given that guy in the knife-edge pants a swift kick in the rear.

But it was too beautiful a day to let a nasty look get to me. I was tempted to walk up the red-carpeted center steps of the elaborate entrance, past the huge white columns and ornate brass lampposts, right into the hotel. What would they do, throw me out? But I just mingled with the crowd outside, trying to act as if I belonged. The world-famous rock star in his jeans and dirty sneakers, waiting for *his* limo. I watched the stream of yellow cabs and gray and silver Cadillacs pull up and leave, while the uniformed attendants, dressed up like naval officers, gold braid and all, opened doors and stacked luggage and greased the way. Overhead, flags rippled in the breeze. I noticed the Italian flag, probably for a dignitary staying at the hotel. In the old days, my father used to have these little flag emblems on the back of our car: a French emblem for Mom and an Italian one for himself. It was Napoleon, he'd said, who changed the blue to green to make the Italian flag from the French tricolor. Everything reminds me of my father, sometimes.

And there was Kelly, early for a change, coming across from Grand Army Plaza with her guitar strapped to her back and the red bandana around her forehead. Heads turned as she walked toward me. I realized all over again how great she looked in her hippie-dippie outfit, with her long hair and green eyes and confident glow.

We did a high five for the limousine crowd, while a doorman all in red gave us a cold-fish stare. I am very sensitive to categories of stares when I'm on alien turf.

"We can try setting up over there," said Kelly, pointing toward the huge square near the hotel. We strolled over, but there were two groups already competing for the crowds, one in front of the big shiny statue of Sherman on his horse, and the other behind the statue, toward Central Park. If we entered the battle, we would overlap them.

The group in front was playing South American folk music on wooden flutes and guitars and a drum. They wore serapes over their denims. They sounded very authentic to me, and they played beautifully. We forgot all about our own gig and watched them for over half an hour. At the end of their long set, we each put a dollar in their guitar case.

"Dynamite!" Kelly said to them. "I saw you guys in the subway last week."

"Yes, yes, miss!" one of them answered. "You were singing, too! Such a voice! You learn Andes music, you can join us!"

A jolt of jealousy hit me. I could lose her so easily, both as a friend and as a music partner. How long would she want to stick with a run-of-the-mill guitarist like me? She *was* good. I felt sick.

"Hey, Kelly," I said weakly. "Maybe we ought to do our own gig now. . . ."

"Oh, right! But not here. It's all taken. And up by the park, there, it's all taken, too."

"We could head for the zoo—"

"How about the subway, Anthony? You said you would."

I must admit I'm a little claustrophobic. I hate being underground. And the subway is so depressing; I usually rush up the stairs to get out as fast as I can. But I had agreed.

"Okay, if you really want to," I said.

"I do! It's fun. You can sing really loud down there. In fact, you have to. Come on, let's try it awhile. We'll sing to the real New Yorkers who come up to the light of day only once a year."

The best station, according to Kelly, was the IRT at Lexington Avenue and Forty-second Street. It was an express stop, with a connection to Times Square. We took the downtown train at Fifty-ninth Street and got off at Forty-second. The station was surprisingly cool, which was a big plus. We set up just inside the underpass to the Times Square shuttle, and switched guitars again. We used Kelly's nice, clean guitar cover to collect the money. She had been right. The crowds rushing along the huge corridor seemed endless; it was like playing to the cars in the Holland Tunnel.

We did very short pieces more or less continually, brief versions of some of our loudest and liveliest stuff. My zoo song, the Beatles' "Octopus's Garden," worked beautifully here. If we weren't under the sea, we certainly were under the ground. Kelly was right, again; the money was good. A lot of people tossed quarters into the open guitar cover as they went by, without stopping. I felt they were treating us as if we were begging; we could have been hitting two frying pans together. But Kelly said they could hear our music all the way back at the entry turnstiles and change booth.

Some people stopped, including a few hood types who looked ready to mug us. One of them seemed drunk or spaced out on drugs. He walked toward us, then staggered away, then back again, over and over, eyeing the money accumulating in Kelly's guitar cover. I nudged Kelly between songs and suggested we change our location.

"Don't worry, Anthony," she said. "If he takes any money, it means he needs it more than we do."

"Aren't you afraid of anybody?"

"Oh, sure. I'm afraid of you."

"What!"

"Yes. I am." The noisy echoing tunnel forced us to yell.

"I don't get it!"

"I'll explain later. Let's sing! We owe it to the world, Tony-Anthony!"

We sang for another hour and a half. Then I cracked, just as the rush hour began. I couldn't take it anymore. I was feeling nauseous. I couldn't handle all the noise and smells and crowds rushing by, and the tunnel closing around me. I cracked. We had come to the end of a Tina Turner song and I shouted to Kelly, "I quit! Please! Kelly! Let's get out of here!"

"You look white."

"I feel sick. I mean it. I'm going to throw up if we don't get out!"

"Okay! Gig ended! Man the hatches! We're surfacing!"

I felt better the moment we hit the street. I wanted to walk awhile, so we headed back uptown. As we walked, my nausea started changing to hunger. It was after five and I hadn't had anything since breakfast. Mom had prepared pancakes and sausage for her last day of rehearsal; it was her way of proving to me and herself that she was normal, relaxed, and sane. I wish Kelly could have first met her flipping those great pancakes, rather than half boozy on Saturday night.

"Say, Kelly," I said, as we walked back up Lexington. "How about feeding the body. I'm the one who's starved this time. I'll treat you with my big earnings."

"Dutch, Tony Anthony. You want to have a picnic?"

"You mean right here on the street?"

"Come on, Anthony. Get real. We go to Gristedes, see, and buy some rolls and Swiss cheese and sliced ham, and let's see, potato salad, cole slaw, chocolate milk, you name it. Then we go into the park—I know a good private spot—and we spread out all the paper and stuff, and make a complete mess. You end up eating potato salad with your fingers. Doesn't that sound great?"

"Not bad. How about Southern fried chicken instead?"

"Anthony, do you really want to know why I like you?"

"Yes."

"Because you're a pig-out specialist, just like me. Let's do it!"

Our picnic was as messy as Kelly said, but it was the most fun I'd had in a long time. We got eight pieces of chicken and a lot of other glop, including the chocolate milk. Kelly had this hidden grassy knoll near my side of the park, in a wild section called the Ramble. There's little bridges and hills and all kinds of narrow paths, with views of the lake below. I wouldn't go there after dark, but it was safe in the evening. I thought.

The food tasted twice as good outdoors, even if we had to wipe our hands on the paper bags. Every so often people passed by; they all seemed in a hurry to get somewhere, even along these winding scenic paths. New Yorkers always rush, particularly at the dinner hour.

As Kelly threw her head way back to drink the last of the chocolate milk, I put my arm around her. Then I made my move as only A. Milano can.

"Give me a chocolate mustache," I said.

Kelly leaned over and gave me a very good kiss. And I moved closer still.

"Anthony, we really should talk," she said.

"You always keep wanting to talk."

"You want to make out, is that it?"

"Well, now that you put it so bluntly—yes."

"We can't do anything in the middle of Central Park. We're right out in the open."

"There's bushes all around us."

"Come on. Everybody can see. Look! Over there. If we can see those people, then they can see us."

"Okay. Talk."

"Don't you want to know why I'm afraid of you?"

"Oh, right. Let's see. Because I punch people out at parties?"

"Very funny. Okay. Here's why. It's because you're making it tough for me to do what I want to do."

"Huh?"

"To be the new me. To quit everything and take off. I'm shaky enough about it, and now you've come along—"

"You don't look shaky about anything to me."

"Well, I am. I put on a good front. I'm famous for my good fronts. But I'm scared of everything. Of my parents. Yes, of them. And of being on my own. And now the worst, of going to the West Coast and losing you completely. See?"

"You'll find someone just as good. Better. It should be easy."

"You *would* say that. Well, you're wrong. You're

really different. You are. Like the way you were with your mother, Saturday night."

"Like a wimp?"

"No! Like a really sweet guy. You care a lot about her; I can tell. And she—I can tell—she really l-loves you. . . ." Tears were suddenly welling up in her eyes.

"I guess she does. . . . Kelly? Why are you crying?"

"Because!" Some tears were going down her cheeks.

"Tell me. What is it? Please!"

"I want to tell you. I really do! But it means—I know it sounds crazy to you—it means giving up what I want to be. Or maybe not. I'm not sure. I'm so confused!"

"Kelly, you know you can tell me anything. Anything."

"I can and I can't. Why did I have to meet you just *now*? Why couldn't you have just been a shit!" She seemed angry.

"Hey, come on. It's not my fault."

"I know. It's the way things break. It's— I guess I need some time to really think about what I'm doing, and about you and me. I— Anyway, that's why I'm afraid of you. Maybe *afraid*'s the wrong word. But you know what I mean. I'm really falling for you, Tony-Anthony. I am. I am."

"And me for you," I said.

"Oh, God, I know. I . . ."

She was looking past me, toward the path. "Uh-oh . . ."

I followed her eyes. Out on the nearby path, two guys, one with a red beard and one blond, were staring at us. That's another thing you don't do: You don't sing on top of someone, and you don't stare at couples obviously trying to be alone.

They didn't move. They looked like bikers without their bikes, in black leather vests and pants and belts and bracelets. One of them, Redbeard, had tattoos all over his arms. I was on ready alert.

I said quietly to Kelly, "Let's, maybe, get up slowly and clear things up and—"

"Yo, blondie!" said Redbeard to Kelly. "You got a nice bod. You ever use it?"

"L-leave us alone," I said, feeling an electric shock of fear and anger. It had been dumb to be in this part of the park this late!

"Hey, listen to Wimpy! You been eating your spinach, Wimpy?"

"That ain't Wimpy. That's Popeye," said Blondbeard.

"Who the hell cares! I like your guitar, blondie," said Redbeard. "It's nice, just like your ass. Which one do I get first?" He walked slowly toward her.

What Redbeard didn't know—what I didn't really know—is that there's something in me that gets triggered, and then I don't think, I don't feel anything, I just go for it. The pot of anger in me boils over—explodes!—like a pressure cooker gone haywire. I leaped up and swung at Redbeard with everything I had, taking him by surprise. He stumbled against some roots and fell clear off the path. My fist ached from the shot.

Kelly screamed. And can she scream! She swung her guitar at Blondbeard, but he jumped away. He grabbed the guitar and started twisting it from her hands. Redbeard was recovering, and I gave him a kick right to the head. It was lunacy, but I did it. He fell back down. I didn't care if it was fair or not. I felt lucky that we were ahead, so far. That we were alive. I prayed that they didn't have knives. Or guns.

I turned toward Blondbeard, but it was too late. He swung at Kelly and hit her below her right eye. She fell against a tree, striking the back of her head. She lay there, stunned. She was bleeding, but I couldn't help her. Blondbeard was coming toward me, still holding Kelly's guitar. I tackled him low, and we both went down. As we wrestled on the ground, I heard some people shouting from farther down the path. Blondbeard managed to twist completely around and throw me off. He shouted to Redbeard, who was half up again, "Let's get the hell outta here!"

As the people got closer, Blondbeard and Redbeard took off, still holding Kelly's guitar. They stumbled down a steep slope to a lower path, then started running out toward Central Park West.

I sank down next to Kelly. She was still bleeding. I tore off the bottom of my T-shirt and pressed it against her cheek. She was shivering, I guess from shock. Three or four people were around us now.

"Call the police!" said a woman in red sweats.

"Are you okay?" I asked

"I'm—I'm f-fine," said Kelly.

"Police!" the woman shouted. "Police!"

"Don't call the—the police," said Kelly. "They'll n-never catch them. And I'm f-fine." She struggled to stand up.

"Are you sure you're all right, miss?" a man asked.

"Y-yes. I'm okay. Please. Don't call the p-police."

We started walking slowly, and I guess it proved to everyone that Kelly was all right. The people offered to help once more, then left.

"Walk me out to—to Fifth Avenue and I'll get a cab," Kelly said. She still held the piece of torn T-shirt against her cheek.

"No! I'm going all the way home with you! I don't give a damn how your house looks."

"Please. Please, Anthony."

"No! Enough's enough, Kelly! I'm walking you home. Or we'll take a cab. Or whatever you want. I'm going with you. And maybe to a doctor."

"I'm okay. Just to the Fifth Avenue side of the—"

"No! If you don't let me go with you, I swear, Kelly, I'll never see you again!"

She looked resigned and grim. "Okay, let's get out of the park," she said.

As we walked slowly toward the park exit, I asked Kelly again and again whether she was sure she was all right.

"It's nothing, Anthony. It's only blood."

"Very nice blood. You were as brave as hell."

"Thanks. So were you. Wow! You could have been killed!"

"I'm sorry about your guitar," I said, feeling like a sudden hero in her eyes. But I was no hero, just momentarily nuts.

"I've got another guitar," she said. "No problem."

When we reached Fifth Avenue, Kelly tried to get rid of me again. She would not give up.

"No! I'm going with you!"

"Okay . . . Anthony, could we sit there a minute?" We went over to one of the benches along the park wall on Fifth Avenue and sat. Kelly leaned back for a moment, studying the tops of some buildings across the street. She sighed and turned toward me.

"This is what—what I was going to tell you," she said. "We won't have to walk far. Because I live right there." She pointed to a building across the street, one of three huge apartment houses. "It's the one we went up."

"What? You mean the place where your mother works? Are you, like, using it while they're away?"

"No. It's . . . I'm sorry, Anthony. It's that my name isn't really Kelly Callahan. My name's Kelsey. You know? Kelsey Lawrence. I'm sorry . . . I'm sorry . . ."

10

IT WAS GETTING DARK. I sat in numbed silence while Kelly—Kelsey?—stared at the sidewalk. Was she giving me another story, like with that guy in San Francisco? Her eyes were tearing again, and her face looked tight as a fist, as if she were fighting to keep control. It didn't seem like a story this time.

"I'm s-sorry," she said again, with a half sob. My world had turned upside down and it was dizzying. That magnificent Fifth Avenue apartment, she belonged in it! It was hers! No wonder she knew so much about the Lawrences' paintings, and their charity donations, and everything. But why couldn't she tell me? She must have been laughing at me all along! Her father was a janitor! Some janitor! Yes, I was angry. But she looked so miserable sitting there, like a kid caught in a petty theft who didn't know what was going to happen next. With her swollen cheek, and the tears, and her tangled hair, I wanted to shake her and hug her at the same time. So she was rich, so what! She was just Kelly to me.

"Hey," I said gently, putting my arm around her. "Take it easy, okay? I'm not going to send you down to the principal's office—"

"Oh, Anthony . . ." She started crying harder now, I held her close and kept repeating, "It's okay. It's okay." Passersby looked, then quickly stared straight ahead.

After a minute or two, her crying eased off. I didn't have any tissues or handkerchief, so I tore off another piece of the bottom of my T-shirt, dirty though it was, and handed it to Kelly. "Blow your nose," I said. And lo and behold, she started laughing at the same time that she was still giving out some sobs. She was a total mess of tears, and sobs, and hurt laughter, and a bruised face, with snot running down from her nose, and I wished I could hold her and comfort her forever.

"Oh God, oh God, Anthony. Only you could do this." She held up my T-shirt rag. "I love you, you nut."

"That's what I was about to say to you—Kelly? Kelsey?"

"Kelly. Please!" She blew her nose, loudly, with my T-shirt scrap, and we both laughed. "See! *Kelsey* wouldn't do that!"

"Okay. *Kelly* . . . That picture you showed me? That wasn't your mother, right?"

"That was my nanny, when I was a little kid. Nans,

I call her. Now she's Andrew's nanny. My kid brother. Her name *is* Callahan. Peggy Callahan. Actually, Pegeen. She doesn't have any kids of her own."

"But she *is* in Europe?"

"Yes. With my parents and Andrew, just like I said. They'll be back in a couple of weeks."

"You could have told me all this. You should have!"

"I swore I was going to be Kelly Callahan. Forever. I want to leave before they get back. I *do* have a friend in San Francisco. She's great; she's already done what I want to do. My parents don't know anything about her. They'll never find me. I'll call them, but they won't know from where."

"Still, you should have told me!"

"I thought about telling you. It's like, at first, I didn't want to blow my cover. I wanted to really try to be someone else. To escape. Then, when I saw you liked me as Kelly, I guess I figured you'd be turned off if you found out who I was."

"Why should I be turned off?"

"Look at how I live! Besides, there's more things . . ."

"And you're not going to tell me, right?" I was feeling an edge of anger again. There was always more, and yet more. It was like peeling an onion.

"I'll tell you. I may as well, now. But you won't like what you hear. You won't."

"Try me!"

"We may as well go up to my place, first. We can get cleaned up, and I could use some ice for my cheek."

"I don't know. . . . Are you sure it's okay?"

"Of course," said Kelly. "There's nobody there. Caitlin's off. Caitlin's our maid. But I still want to use the service entrance. All I need is Arthur seeing me like this."

"Arthur?"

"The night doorman."

We went up to her apartment complex just as before, but everything felt different now. She was slumming, going up this way. That elegant glass-and-marble front entrance was hers to use if she wanted. Arthur would tip his cap to her. The limos I'd seen in front of the Plaza, those were hers to use, too, if she wished. I always thought people who lived in these Fifth Avenue apartments were practically another species. But she was so down-to-earth; she had no airs at all. Was that just her Kelly transformation? As we went up in the service elevator, I decided to try to be cool, as if all this super-wealth meant nothing to me. But did it? I wasn't sure.

The huge dining room seemed overwhelming now, in the dimming light from the giant windows. It wasn't foreign soil anymore, somebody else's castle. It was hers! She lived in it, ate in it, breathed in it. Her father was a janitor! That still hurt. She should have told me! She should have!

We went through the dining room to the bathroom to wash. Even the bathroom was magnificent. It was larger than my mother's bedroom, with twin sinks, a dressing room, and an oversized sunken square tub with a TV set and a stereo to one side. The toilet was neatly tucked away in its own separate room. And there was another open area with a Jacuzzi. All hers. Kelly-Kelsey's.

I studied my face in the large mirror above the sinks. I was surprised to see that my face was filthy and covered with some long scratches I hadn't even felt.

"I think we were lucky to get out of this alive," I said.

"I think you're right," said Kelly as she poked her cheek. "This is pretty swollen already. I guess it's too late for ice. . . . Relax, Anthony. It's like I said, this place is just a garbage dump with brass trimmings."

"Some dump," I said. "This is what it's all about, for most people."

"Is it for you?"

"No."

"That's another thing. I could never make friends with people who didn't live like this. I never could tell whether they liked me for myself. You know the way it is. So with you, I knew it was for me. Just me. . . . Even with my own crowd, there were always a lot of power plays going on. Some of them are okay; I've got to be fair. But even at best—like Michelle, you saw her in the park, that day, remember?—she's stuck in the city weekdays doing work for her father. He owns some hotels. Anyway, even she thinks I'm some kind of traitor because I stopped going to our old hangouts. I eased off in the spring and quit completely in May. Michelle doesn't understand."

We went back into the dining room and sprawled out on some of the huge cushions. They were amazingly comfortable.

"Is that why she was so sore at you?" I asked.

"I guess. She just won't *let* herself understand. Because if she did, she'd be admitting something's wrong with all of us. She can't see that I'm sick of going to those expensive bars where they look the other way at your ID's, and the drinks cost five dollars each. I'm sick of going for the next hot drug. First it was coke, then it was crack, now it's ecstasy. Coke is the big number, but we tried the rest. See? Are you getting the picture, Anthony? I got sick of ending up with a different guy every couple of months. Or weeks. Or even days. Okay, Anthony? Is that what you wanted to hear? Well, that's how it was. Don't look like that! I told you you wouldn't like it. But that's the way it was. Weekend lunches with my mother or aunt at Le Cirque, or Lutece, or Le Bernardin, or some other three- or four-star restaurant—all very nice, *Vanity Fair* and *Vogue*-ish—and nights with my friends, sniffing and snorting and smoking anything and everything, and getting drunk as skunks, and doing the discos till morning, and playing musical bodies—Okay, Anthony? Okay? How's that?"

"What—what about your parents?" I asked weakly. "I mean, didn't they care or—"

"Oh, yes, my parents. At first, it was all so With It! And Now! And Swinging! So long as it was nicely under control, right? I think my mother loved the idea that I was doing all this stuff behind her back with all the other power kids, spaced out on—on absolutely empty nothing! Her questions were almost like voyeurism, when she bothered to ask questions. I think she envied me! Because she couldn't do this when she was a kid. Her parents were poor, back in England, but strict as hell. As for my father, he might just as well have been on the moon. And then, when it got to be a real problem, they started acting as if I were some kind of criminal. My mother was so angry that, at one point, she almost lost her upper-class British accent, but not quite. . . . They're such phonies. They say they care. But if they really cared, they wouldn't be in England right now. For all they know, I could be doing coke again.

"Well, Anthony? How do you like your Kelly in the windblown tree now? It's good-by, Anthony, right? Right? You can go out the front entrance and give Arthur a swift kick in the you-know-what for me. Good old Arthur. He's been trying to come on to me. Nice, huh? When they see you come home at six in the morning, then they think you're a target. And they're right. I started using the service elevator because of that. I had to sneak in because of the doorman, not my parents. How's that for a laugh? I—Good-by, Anthony! Right? Right? It's good-by, right?"

She looked totally miserable, sitting on a beige cushion with her bruised face and eyes swollen from all the crying. No wonder she wanted to change her life. No wonder. She folded her arms up tight against her body as if to protect herself from an attacker. Her hair was over her face in strings. I swear she looked like a beaten animal, wanting not to be kicked again. Her eyes were begging me. But as far as I was concerned, Kelly—not Kelsey, Kelly!—was born the day I met her. To hell with that other garbage. So I'm crazy, but that's how I felt.

"Bullshit to good-by," I said. "I don't care about that other stuff. I mean, I care, because it's hurt you so much. But it doesn't make me feel any different. Maybe it should, but it doesn't. I admit, I wish those guys could be wiped out of the world by magic, somehow—but that's gone. Right? That's over. And—and I'm right here. I'm now."

"Anthony . . . you are something else. . . . Oh, God. . . ." She was crying all over again. I held her tight, like before, feeling sorry for her, and maybe for me, and for the whole world. And I understood how Kelly could care about all those derelicts she helped, because she looked like a derelict herself, so alone, wrapping herself in her arms like a shield. And I'm not ashamed; we cried together, Kelly and me, cried, and held each other, and sat still finally, breathing together. We were alone, together, in this dark spaceship above Manhattan, alone, just us, in the universe. Never again, ever, will there be anything more close and good to me than our breath on each other's faces in the dark, without words.

11

THREE DIFFERENT CLOCKS in Kelly's apartment struck ten at almost the same moment. We went outside to the terrace and sat in the dark, watching the headlights come down Fifth Avenue and the thousands of red taillights stream away. There was a *yip-yip* of sirens in the distance as the stars came out above the massive buildings across Central Park. It was like being in a movie; all glitz and glass behind us and New York City out there, surrounding us. We started talking about anything and everything, the way I sometimes talked to Jason. Our voices seemed detached from our bodies.

In the dark, it was easier for me to tell Kelly about my father and how he'd suddenly left us. And how I missed him. I rambled on about Mom and the theater and how I met Jason. I even told her about that stage-prop snake. And she told me about their house in Newport, Rhode Island, and their huge sailboat and the yacht club they belonged to, and how everyone always competed, not just with racing, but with the size and cost of their boats, and their construction and fixtures, right down to the electronics and radio equipment. Everything her family did was a contest to get ahead, to be first, to be in. There was no time to stop and just *be*. Or to really notice her, Kelly-Kelsey.

"What saved me was the music," Kelly said, very softly. "When I was down—I mean in the total dumps—when I was sick of doing coke or pot, I'd play some chords on the guitar and sing to myself. It helped."

"I know; I've done the same thing," I said. "It's like having a friend with you, right there."

"And when you're down, your friend is down. And when you're up, your friend is up. Like a twin sister or brother."

"Right." She understood how I felt better than Jason ever did. For a second, I thought of *her* as my twin sister.

"Sometimes," she said, "I'd play my tapes and records, but usually I sang. For hours and hours. Classical stuff, too. Arias. *'Spargi d'amaro pianto'* from *Lucia.* Or *'Addio del passato'* from *Traviata.* All the sad stuff. Do you like opera?"

"I don't know. I don't know much about it."

"I've studied for years. The minute I told them I

wanted to sing, it had to be opera, of course. Voice lessons. French lessons. Italian. Sightsinging. On and on. That's what I'm supposed to be doing this summer, they *think*!"

"I should have guessed," I said. "You sound like you've got a trained voice."

She gave a tiny laugh. "Trained? You mean like little dogs dressed in tutus? Or dolphins jumping through hoops? One-two-three, jump!"

"You know what I mean. Your voice really carries."

"I'll say. You know, getting voice training is like getting a nose job. After they're done, it isn't you anymore. That's why most opera stars can't sing a simple pop or jazz or blues piece. They make it all sound like *Lohengrin*. It's almost comical."

"You're feeling better, right?"

"Much. I really, really like being with you, Anthony. You don't play games. No big front. No macho scenes. You're just you . . . Anthony? Tony-Anthony? How about, in two weeks, going to the West Coast with me?"

"I can't. I wish I could. But there's my mother. And school. And a million things . . . Or maybe I don't have the guts."

"Oh, yes you do. You could go. I don't have the guts, either. I'm scared stiff of my parents, for one thing. They're here even when they're not here. But you turn this knob in your head; you turn this knob to *Go*. And you'll go. . . . Will you think about it?"

"Sure. But you could turn a knob in *your* head, to

Stay. And you'd stay."

"I can't. I can't live here anymore. I won't."

"Would *you* think about it?" I asked.

"I've thought about it for months and months—God, I just realized! I'm going to have to stay away from my aunt, with this swollen cheek. See what I mean when I say that I'm still scared of them? I'm supposed to report to her regularly, like a parole officer. That's why I had to split the day we were at the boat pond. You should have seen me run home to change from my street clothes into my goody-goody clothes. She's my warden while they're in England."

"I thought they didn't care what you did."

"They don't. But they can tell everybody, including themselves, that Aunt Carol is keeping an eye on me. Actually, she's going to Newport on Wednesday; she's having an affair. Hooray! Nice, huh? My uncle doesn't know. But I do. She told me at one of our cozy little lunches. I guess she needs a parole officer, too."

"Like my father . . . I wish my mother would find someone else. So she could let go of . . ."

"What?"

"Nothing."

"Let go of you?"

"No, of *him*. Finally." But it *was* me! My face felt hot. She could read me like an open book with oversized letters.

"How about, both of you?"

"I don't know. Maybe. But she's had a lot of problems. She can't help it. You sound as if you don't like her."

"No, I do! I understand, Anthony. I do. . . . God, but the world is strange, isn't it? My mother is just the opposite of yours. We should switch mothers. You know, sometimes I actually do feel Nans is my mother. It wasn't that hard for me to pretend. I hope you get to meet her. She's great." She pressed her bruised cheek and winced.

"Is it still hurting?" I asked.

"A little. But I'm feeling much better inside. Thank you, Anthony."

"For what?"

"For being Anthony Milano, instead of someone else. . . . Hey, Anthony! How would you like to go on another picnic tomorrow? A no-mugging picnic, this time. You'll see the sights of New York. The real sights."

"Okay. But where?"

"You'll find out. It'll be a surprise picnic. Don't bring your guitar. I'll take mine, my other one. For picnic music. Can you meet me here tomorrow at, say, eleven? You can come in the front entrance and give Arthur a kiss for me. Or Fred. I think Fred is on duty then. He's just as bad."

"Okay. What can I bring? Some fried chicken?"

"Don't bring anything. It's all going on my credit card. Do you know that I've got a card with a ten-thousand dollar credit limit? Sick, right?"

It was enormous! My mother's card has a two-thousand dollar limit, and she's lucky to have that, the way things are. "But I thought you were giving all that up," I said. "I thought you were quitting."

"I am. I'm not going to use it in San Francisco. But I'm using it here. You bet I am. When I'm done, there's going to be no credit left."

It seemed almost like theft to me. Wasn't that money her parents', not hers? It troubled me. Every time I thought I understood her, every time things seemed smooth, just ahead was yet another Kelly for me to puzzle over. But it was the wrong time to start giving her the third degree, because as we sat there in the dark, watching New York pull down its shades and turn off its lights, I was feeling sexier and sexier.

I moved closer to her and gave her a clumsy kiss. We hugged and started touching each other here and there, and kissed some more and touched some more. But then she moved my hand away and said no, no, she wanted it to be different with me.

"I did too much with too many guys. I don't know how to say this—I want everything right and special. I don't want to just flop into bed. I don't know; maybe I need a shrink. It's, like, I connect sex with doing coke. I was always high. But it'll come. Just don't be like those guys. Don't push me. Let me decide when. Please?"

"Anything," I said. "Whatever you want. Can't I even kiss you?"

"Oh, of course. Yes! Only *you* could ask something like that! You're so—God! Like I said. Why couldn't you just be a shit, like the other guys! It would make my life so easy!"

"Is that what you want?"

"No . . . no . . . but I've got to get away. And you're here."

"We'll figure something out."

"Maybe."

"You gotta have faith. Remember?"

"Oh, that old thing. Right. Right."

"We'll figure something out. We will." I wished I could really believe it.

12

IT WAS CLOSE TO MIDNIGHT when I got home. I took a cab across the park; what the hell. It cost four dollars and thirty cents. Unfortunately, I didn't have a credit card for ten dollars, let alone ten thousand.

Mom was at the kitchen table drinking only coffee, thank goodness. She was in her old, very theatrical, red silk kimono. She's had it ever since I can remember.

"Where in heaven and earth have you been?" she asked.

"Out. So how was final rehearsal?"

"Disastrous, Anthony. Disastrous. *Out* is no answer. I've wanted to talk to you. I don't think we've had three words since Saturday night."

"Mom, we had breakfast together this morning.

You made pancakes, remember?"

"Yes, but we didn't talk. Perhaps we grunted a bit. Not your fault; that's me in the morning. Anthony, would you be ashamed if I got a job at one of the better shops, Bloomingdale's or Lord and Taylor?"

"No. But why?"

"I must get out of the business. Acting has become a burden. I'm losing my nerve."

"Okay. Maybe you'll be happier."

"Okay? Just *okay*? Is that what I get after thirty years in the theater? Do you know what it means for me to leave?"

"I know! What can I do? I can't give you nerve if you don't have nerve. I don't even know what nerve means, actually."

"It means I'm through!"

"Mom, I'm sor—"

"Martine!"

"Martine, I'm sorry. I don't know what to say. I can't handle it. All I can tell you is that you're always this way before an opening night."

"It's not an opening!"

"It is for you!"

"I'm just stepping into a role."

"You're the whole play."

"What play? It's one short scene. About a failed marriage. Or a sick one, your choice. Either way, I'm typecast."

"Okay. I can't win. I tell you, you'll be fine. Should I come down tomorrow, for the big moment? You don't usually want me around at openings, but . . . what do you think?"

"Why fuss over a stupid twenty-minute sketch? That's it, a sketch. I hate Strindberg for having written the damn thing!"

"I could come with Kelly."

"Kelly? Is that who you were out with? It's none of my business. But I'm sure you were. Did she scratch your face like that? In a fit of glorious passion, my Antonio?"

"No!"

"Well, I must say, she seems like a very nice girl. Isn't she too short for you, though, Anthony?"

"Martine!"

"But she's very *simpàtica.* I like her. See, we haven't even talked about her. Is it, how shall I ask? Serious?"

"We did talk about her. You said you liked her, at breakfast."

"Well, I still do. See how consistent I am? . . . But she's *very* short."

"*Mom!*"

"All right, Anthony! Mothers do notice these things. I suppose in the theater we're forever casting people, and I would not cast her with you, on appearance alone. The audience would titter. It would be distracting."

"Well, I'm as happy as hell that my life isn't a play!"

"Well said. Touché. Touché. I hope you're using protective measures."

"Good grief, Mom—Martine!"

"Because you must never trust the girl for such things. I've said it, and I'm glad."

"Okay, okay."

"I'm going to lose you soon, isn't that so, Anthony? You're almost sixteen. Two more years and—"

"I may not go to college."

"You should. I no longer care to see you in the theater. Study something practical. Be an engineer."

"I'd rather be a decaying corpse in the jungles of Bolivia."

"Two years . . ."

"Martine, it's none of my business, but since you're giving me sex-education lessons, I've wanted to say something for a long time—why don't you, uh, well, start dating someone?"

She laughed out loud and choked on the coffee. I didn't think it was funny. She needed someone besides me. Kelly had put a bug in my ear.

"I may have more of a private life than you know about, Anthony," she said after recovering from her dumb laughing.

"I know your private life. It's sitting in front of the TV with a glass of Chablis."

"Thank you!"

"It's true."

"I have many, many friends. Including males, Anthony. I've had a few bad spells from time to time, that's all."

"A few!"

"All right, Anthony. In case you want to know, Johnny Barnett, the great director himself, has been making passes at me."

"Good."

"In any other business, I could report him for sexual harassment."

"Even better."

"You are getting to be a perfect pain in the butt, Anthony. I'm supposed to be telling *you* what to do. . . . If only he weren't a director. I'm allergic to directors, as you well know. But Johnny and I go back a long way."

"Good. Good. Go out with him. Is he married or anything?"

"Not lately."

"Good. You have my permission. You can go to bed with him. But make sure you have protection. Because you can never trust the man."

"O my oblivion is a very Antony! You are getting to be a very definite butt pain. . . . But I'll give it some thought."

"Please!"

"Why are you so eager?"

"Because . . . because I love you. How's that?"

"A nice line to close an act."

"God! Mom—Martine! You're incurable!"

The phone rang. Mom's face fell half a mile. "Oh, God. You take it, Anthony," she said, waving her hand toward the phone.

We both knew who it was. Dad never seemed to

remember the time difference between the east and west coasts. It was midnight here, but only nine P.M. at his end. When the phone rang this late, it was always Dad.

Perfect timing. Here we were, talking about Mom going out with Johnny Barnett, and bingo! Was Dad into telepathy?

I'm always uptight with Dad on the phone. I don't know what to say; my life is so far away from him now. I lifted the receiver.

"Hello?"

"Hey, Tony. How are you doing, buddy?" It *was* Dad.

"Okay. I'm okay."

"How's your mother?"

"She's pretty good." Mom didn't leave the room; she sat right there, trying to fill in his end of the conversation. She doesn't want to talk to him, but she won't let go of him.

"Well, that's good to hear," said Dad. "The reason I'm calling—ahem—I read in the notices in *Variety* that she's going to step into a play Off-Broadway. And, well, I wanted to wish her luck—ahem—Do you think she'd come to the phone? Ahem—ahem . . ."

Dad has always had this nervous cough from years of cigarettes. When I dream about him—and I still do a lot—I always hear that cough, that *ahem*, in my sleep. Sometimes, if the dream wakes me, I'll sit up in bed and listen to see if his cough has actually come from our living room.

"Tony," Dad repeated, "can she—ahem—come to the phone?"

"Uh—I don't think she's, uh . . ." I pointed toward Mom, who was watching, then to the phone, in a silent question. Mom shook her head no, then mimed being asleep.

"I think she's gone to bed."

"Oh. Well, tell her I wish her a lot of luck, okay, Tony? I mean, hell, she deserves a good break. You know, I've asked her to come out here; I could get her some parts. Ahem. She's a great character actress. But she won't."

"I know."

"I don't want to put you in the middle, buddy, but you ought to talk to her. She doesn't have to see *me*. But I know a lot of people in this business—"

"She hates film acting, Dad."

Mom nodded her approval of my words. She might just as well have gotten on the phone. She was practically a third party on the line.

"So, Tony. How's life been treating you?"

"Okay."

"Did you get that camera I sent you?"

"Oh. Right. It's—really nice. Thanks. I used it for a school project."

"Hey, good. How's the guitar playing?"

"Good. I met this—I've teamed up with a girl I met, and we've been making some money playing in the park, and all."

"That's great. Nice girl?"

"Uh-huh."

"That's good. That's good. But be careful about you-know-what. Ahem. You know what I mean."

"That's just what Mom said before. Be careful."

Mom gave a snort, as if Dad should be the last person to advise me.

"See!" said Dad. "You still have two parents who care about you. That's what's important. I do care about you, Tony. I think about you a lot."

"I know." I couldn't get myself to say I thought about him a lot, too. Certainly not in front of Mom. But I wished I could have.

"So okay, Tony, buddy. I'll call you soon. Think about coming out here. Anytime. Okay?"

"Okay."

"So long, Tiger."

"So long, Dad." I hung up.

Mom looked at me with her mouth shut tight, as if she were definitely *not* going to ask me anything. But I knew she wanted me to talk.

"He said I should wish you luck. He read about your opening in *Variety*."

"Oh."

"And he says he can get you film work if you went out to L.A."

"Well isn't that *kind* of him."

"I'm sorry, Mom. That's what he said. And he asked about my music—well, you heard it all. He said he cares, and all that."

"He does care about you, Anthony. That's why he

keeps calling. I don't take that away from him. He does. We both do."

"That's what he said, too."

"That we both . . ."

"Yes."

"Well . . ." There were tears in her eyes now. "At least we haven't each tried to turn you against the other. That's something. We haven't, have we? *Have* we?"

"No."

"You're the one part of our life that we both—that we both—" She put her hand over her eyes to hide her tears.

"It's okay, Mom."

"That we both . . ."

13

I'D BEEN IN FAIRLY POSH apartment buildings before. For example, Jason's was pretty spectacular if you didn't look too closely at the red carpet in the lobby—which showed its age, especially near the elevators—or the potted trees around the fountain that were losing their leaves in July. Then why was I so totally uptight as I approached Kelly's building?

As I walked through the outer glass doors with their shining brass grillwork, I swallowed so hard the doorman must have heard me. The outer lobby wasn't that elaborate. Marble and brass, but small.

"Kelly—Um, Kelsey Lawrence's apartment, please."

"And your name?"

"Anthony Milano." Did I detect a slight frown?

Were visitors of Italian extraction unacceptable?

He lifted his phone and pressed a couple of buttons. "Fred, here," he said. "A Mr. Anthony Milano for— Yes, very good." He hung up and said to me, "Fourteenth floor. The elevator to the right."

The inner lobby was done in the best of taste. It was far less elaborate than Jason's. No trees, no fountains, just white and pink marble and a deep blue-and-red Persian rug. Some fresh flowers in a large oriental vase. And a modern landscape painted by someone or other.

The elevator I took had only three stop buttons: 12A, 14, and 15. Talk about exclusiveness. I pressed 14 and noticed I was sweating like crazy. The elevator walls were made of inlaid wood, with flower designs along the edges. No scratches anywhere, not even an initial.

At the fourteenth floor, the door slid open and I was in a little upper lobby, all white and pink marble again. There was a heavy wooden door with flowers and deer carved on it in a set of four panels, as if the artwork in the apartment continued outside. I buzzed, waited, then knocked, right on a deer's head.

After the familiar sound of clicking bolts, the door opened. A young woman stood there, dressed as a maid. For a moment I felt as if I were in one of my mother's plays, where all the maids and butlers are actors. But this wasn't a play; she *was* the maid.

"Uh, is Kell—Kelsey here?" I stammered.

"Oh, yes, she's in the kitchen. I'll tell her you're

here. Do come in." The maid zipped off and I walked in awkwardly, feeling like a goon and nervous as hell.

I was in another huge room, with wood paneling, and sofas everywhere, and more paintings, and a kind of greenhouse or solarium at the far end. In a second, Kelly came in, with the maid a few steps behind her.

"Hi, Tony-Anthony. This is Caitlin. She's my buddy."

"Hello," I said, not knowing what you say to an official maid, let alone a buddy.

"How do, sir." She had a kind of British accent, but different.

"Caitlin, I'm going to be out, I think, all day," said Kelly. "So, you know, if my aunt calls, I'm out."

"At classes, Miss?"

"Right. As far as you know."

"Yes, Miss."

"Have fun, Caity. Burn the place down." Caitlin tittered, a little embarrassed, then zipped out of the room again.

"She's great," said Kelly. Then more softly, "She knows I'm not going to voice classes, but she doesn't know about Kelly Callahan. I should have warned you."

"Are there others? I mean, like maids and stuff?"

"They're on vacation, or in England with Nans and the rest. Caitlin's holding the fort. We've gotten to be real friends this summer. Like, I cover for her, and she's able to see her boyfriend a lot more. She's Welsh. Anyway, she's not a maid, Anthony. She's a person. I like her a lot more than some of my so-called friends."

"I can see why. She seems very nice," I said. "Man, this is some room!"

"Oh, this is the oompah-pah living room. You were in the dining room yesterday. But don't worry. We've got roaches in this room, too."

"How's your cheek?" I asked.

"Pretty good. If you kiss it, it'll be even better."

I kissed her on both cheeks. Then I reached around her waist for the real stuff, and we did a Milano special. She pulled away after a moment.

"No more, Tony-Anthony. We've got to get going. Did you have breakfast?"

"Yes."

"Good. Because we're not going to eat for a while. Okay. The stuff's in the other room. Caitlin helped me pick it up this morning from this fancy deli on Lexington. I hope you're feeling strong today."

We went into the dining room, and there on the long glass table were four big shopping bags loaded to the top. It would have taken Napoleon's army to eat all that.

"Are you kidding!" I said.

"Don't panic, friend. It's not all for us."

"Well, but then who?"

"You'll find out. Follow me, Anthony. This time we go out the front. Fred will think evil thoughts if he doesn't see us come out pretty fast. His mind works that way."

The bags weighed a ton, but if my petite Kelly could haul two of them, so could I. And she'd strapped her guitar to her back, too, that other guitar she'd mentioned. Strange; she'd asked me to leave mine home. I waddled toward the door with the two largest bags. From what I could tell, they seemed to be full of sandwiches and fruit and pints of chocolate milk.

We took the elevator down and went out the lobby balanced like a pair of tightrope performers. Fred said a low "Morning, Miss Lawrence" to Kelly. It sounded perfectly polite to me. But he did seem to be staring at her rear as we left, or was it my imagination?

Kelly's next move was another unexpected caper. She put her bags down, walked out into the street, and raised her hand to hail a cab. It was the way she did it, as if she had been born to summon cabs. A bit of the Lawrence side of her coming through? Like a shot, Fred was out there. "I'll do that, Miss." He raised a white-gloved hand, then put a thin silver whistle to his mouth and blew an ear-splitting *twee-twee!* A cab swung toward us and stopped at the curb, in front of the little iron ramp that kept people from parking there.

"This is the best way, with all these bags," Kelly said as Fred and the cabby loaded our stuff into the trunk. We slid into the rear seat with its torn leather covering. Kelly called out, "The Starlight Hotel."

"Sorry, sweetheart," the cabby said. "Don't know

where that one is."

"Oh. Forty-fourth near Ninth."

A picnic in a hotel? It was getting nuttier by the minute. And what kind of hotels were down on Ninth Avenue and Forty-fourth Street? Not the Plaza, I'll tell you.

The ride was like most cab trips in Manhattan: the bronco-buster special. By the time we arrived at the hotel, I didn't think I could eat anything, even if my life depended on it. Riding cabs in the Big Apple is a good way to diet.

The Starlight Hotel was not starry; it was miserably run-down. As we went inside, it dawned on me: This was the Kelly of the giveaway dollar bills, in action again. The lobby smelled of urine, plain and simple. Maybe it was a hotel, but there was no doorman, no manager, nobody. But there was an elevator.

Kelly pushed the *Up* button and the elevator door rumbled open. Inside the elevator, propped up against the back wall, was a man with a bandaged head and no shoes. He looked drunk; we could smell his breath in the lobby.

"Lemmee alone!" he called. "This is my house! This is my house!"

"Okay," Kelly said. "Sorry." She nodded toward the stairs. "Come on, Anthony. We can walk. It's only three flights."

The stairs and landings were covered with litter. There were tiny metal bottles and small transparent envelopes and little glass vials everywhere. On the second landing two men, maybe in their thirties, were leaning against a wall.

"You think it's safe?" I whispered to Kelly.

"Sure. They're just nodding out on something. This is drug alley, here. They come off the street. It's not good, especially for the kids who live here."

"Is this a welfare hotel?"

"You got it, Tony-Anthony."

"It looks really bad."

"It *is* bad. The city's trying to move everybody to permanent apartments, but it's slow. And some of those apartments are worse than this hotel."

We pushed the fire door open on the third floor; the long hallway was full of kids. Two or three were riding tricycles up and down; one was on roller skates; some girls were jumping rope. They were all over the place. Some of the kids were sitting on the mangy green carpet runner, playing with cards and blocks and some pretty grungy dolls. The kids were every color and race: African American, white, Hispanic, Asian. A United Nations of poverty.

"They've made the third floor the playground," said Kelly. "Their moms are afraid to let them play in the street. It's dangerous around here. This way, they take turns watching them."

At the far end, I saw a woman, no doubt one of the mothers, trying to sew something while keeping an eye on the kids. We walked slowly down the long corridor, stepping around the seated children.

"Hi, Kelly," one little girl said.

"Hi, Donna. Where's your sister?"

"She's sick."

Most of the kids looked happy enough, but a few sat by themselves, staring at the wall or the floor. Kelly put down her bags for a moment and lifted a boy's head up, gently.

"You okay, Darryl?" she asked.

"Yeah."

"You sure?"

"Yeah."

"You going to come to my picnic?"

"I dunno."

"Well, please come. Okay?"

"Okay."

We walked over to the woman who was sewing. "Hi, Mrs. Turner. This is my friend Anthony."

"Well, it must be Tuesday," said Mrs. Turner. "Just like clockwork. You look like you got plenty of good things there."

"Chicken salad and ham salad, today."

"Sounds good. What'd they do to your cheek, girl?"

"Oh, I walked into a mugger's fist."

"Lord! It is the end of the world coming! You see that bum in the elevator?"

"We sure did."

"Can't get him out. We called the owner and he don't care. The man's *living* there. He keeps coming back. Can't let the kids go in the elevator no more. Yesterday he exposed himself. Smell that lobby? That's him."

"Why—why not call the police?" I asked.

She gave me a long look. "We don't call the police here if we can help it."

Kelly started bustling around with Mrs. Turner's help. They got two beat-up card tables out of a couple of rooms, and some other mothers joined us to help set things up. The kids didn't look all that interested until Kelly started piling up the containers of chocolate milk and a million wrapped vanilla cupcakes.

"Hey, it's Kelly!" one of the boys shouted. "She got us chocolate milk!"

Within five minutes, the corridor was mobbed. Word had traveled through the building, and more kids came down, some with mothers, some alone. As the women handed out sandwiches and milk and fruit and cupcakes, Kelly started strumming her guitar. "Let's do a couple, Anthony," she said. She handed me the guitar, and we launched into our South Street Seaport act, as best we could in the corridor. I must admit, it was fun. No one, of course, gave us money, and I liked that most of all. I was doing something good for a change, and it felt terrific.

As the kids went back to playing their games, we had a couple of sandwiches ourselves, and some of the milk. The food was really good. But even with all the people there, two of the bags were still full. I asked Kelly about it as I finished my second cupcake.

"More stops to make," said Kelly. "Okay, Mrs. Turner. We've got to go. We're heading downtown."

"You take care," said Mrs. Turner.

"Have you heard from Mrs. Ortiz yet? The apartment she got isn't that great, but it's right by a school."

"She's lucky."

"That's the people I helped move Sunday, Anthony. They got permanent housing. She got a job, too."

"She's real lucky," said Mrs. Turner. "Real lucky."

"You'll get lucky, too."

"Maybe. Maybe not."

"I'll see you next Tuesday, Mrs. Turner. If it's okay?"

"Sure it's okay. We ain't going nowhere. If it makes you feel good—"

"I wish I could do more," said Kelly apologetically.

"Your heart's in the right place, girl. But it'll take a lot more than sandwiches to straighten this mess out. This *mess*!" She waved her hand upward, as if to mean the entire building. Or the whole world.

"I know," said Kelly softly. "I'm sorry."

"So am I, honey. So am I."

We went down the stairs, silently, past the guys doing drugs, out the smelly lobby to the street.

"Well," said Kelly as we walked toward Broadway, "now you know what I'm doing with that credit I told you about. As long as it lasts."

I was relieved to hear it. I'd really thought, last night, that she meant to waste the money, just to spite her parents. "They didn't seem all that enthusiastic," I said. "I mean, like Mrs. Turner."

"How would you feel, having to get handouts? At

least it saves them some food stamps once a week. I don't know . . . now you've got me thinking. Maybe Mrs. Turner is right. Maybe I'm just doing this for myself. To make me feel good."

"Maybe. But you could really do a tremendous amount, someday."

"Oh? How?"

"When all the stuff your parents have is yours."

"You're dreaming. That'll be a million years from now. Besides, they'll probably disinherit me."

"Or you could try to make them do more, right now."

"I've tried. Plenty. You don't know them. My God, they're going to be back in less than two weeks! I've got to really start making plans for Splitsville."

"But wouldn't it be better to keep on trying rather than just quit?"

"Oh, great! You've found a firecracker to throw at me!"

"No. It's just—maybe all I want is to keep you here."

"Come with me!"

"I can't."

"We're going in circles, Anthony. Can we cool it?"

"Sure."

"Okay . . . I'm going to get us a cab again. We've still got these two bags. Ready for more action, Anthony?"

"Aye, aye, sir."

She gave the cab driver a street corner way downtown, Lafayette Street and Franklin. And we were on our way again, zooming down Broadway in our yellow submarine, squeezing between cars and buses, and jumping traffic lights like crazy. We zigged and zagged on the downtown streets and ended up in a business district with high buildings and open plazas. Why would Kelly want to bring sandwiches here? As we walked along Franklin Street, I asked her point-blank.

"You'll see. There's some really tough cases down here. Someone at the Starlight told me about this place. She calls it the Cardboard Condominium."

I didn't understand what Kelly meant until we turned the corner and walked into a plaza with an arcade at one side. And there it was, two long lines of huge cardboard boxes, the kind they use for big appliances like refrigerators. Some boxes were under the arcade and some were out in the open, and there were people living there, right inside the boxes. They'd furnished them, crudely, with old cushions, mattresses, blankets, and crates. Some of the men were in pretty bad shape. There were a couple of women, too.

It reminded me of a movie I'd seen about Calcutta. It felt unreal, like a stage set, this cardboard village in the middle of these Manhattan office buildings. But it was real. And nobody seemed to care.

Kelly gave me her guitar to hold and, without a word, went from box to box, handing out food. A few of the men thanked her, but one spat toward her. He held an open knife in his hand. He seemed drunk and dazed as he played with the knife, chopping the air with it. I was scared out of my wits for Kelly. But she just put her sandwich and milk and cupcake down, then said, "Have a good day." She turned toward me, shrugged her shoulders, and smiled. Talk about laid-back!

The guy kept playing with the knife, and her back was toward him as she moved to the next box. I was ready to jump him if he moved. Kelly didn't seem the least bit worried.

Was this courage? Saintliness? Stupidity? Or maybe being rich, she'd never felt endangered, despite what happened to us in the park. I didn't know. But I knew that I'd never forget the cool, calm way she moved that afternoon, among those wrecked men. One of them had his pants half off. It was terrible; embarrassing and ugly at the same time. His body was filthy. Kelly put down a sandwich, a cupcake, fruit, and milk.

"Have a good afternoon," she said.

"God bless ya."

"You, too."

There seemed to be something inside Kelly that was as tough as iron, or gentle as a flower, or both; something I couldn't understand. Maybe that's why she could go to the West Coast, while I couldn't. She kept giving out the food, not looking back, not afraid at all, and it was, like, almost religious. I couldn't believe that the girl I was watching had gone to bed with a million guys, had done all kinds of drugs, had done the disco scene all night. Had cried in my arms.

More men appeared from around the block, and she handed food out to all of them. Not one of them tried to insult her, or come on to her, or anything. They seemed in awe. *I* was in awe. Within ten minutes, there was no food left.

As we walked east along White Street, my curiosity spilled over. "How . . . That guy with the knife. Weren't you afraid?"

"No . . ."

"But he could have stabbed you!"

"He wouldn't have. Besides, you were there, Tony-Anthony."

"I'm not always there! Good grief!"

"Why are you so angry?"

"Because you could get killed!"

"Well, if I did, it would be a very small funeral. You and Nans."

"You know that's not true!"

"Yeah . . ."

We were passing Columbus Park, the block-sized park at the edge of Chinatown. "Let's go in," said Kelly. We strolled over to a bench opposite a long brick building with a covered stage. Little kids, mostly Chinese, were playing with toy trucks and cars. Their mothers, on a nearby bench, spoke to each other in Chinese, but the kids all spoke English.

"God, they're so cute," said Kelly. "Someday I want

to have a lot of kids. If I can ever straighten myself out."

"You seem pretty straightened out, doing all these things here and at the Starlight Hotel."

"No, I'm not. I'm a lot more messed up than you think." As she studied the kids playing, she looked defeated suddenly, all drawn into herself, like my mother when she's down. I waited awhile, but she kept staring at the kids.

"Kelly," I said gently, "I guess you still didn't tell me everything, right?" Not too hard to guess.

"Right." After a moment, she sighed and shrugged her shoulders. "It's no big deal. It's—well, I tried to kill myself last year. I feel so weird, saying it."

"Oh, God."

"No, it's okay. I'm here. I messed it up, like everything else. . . . My parents don't even know."

"How could they not know!"

"Easy." She was silent again, staring at the kids.

"Please, Kelly. You keep stopping; like you don't trust me, or something. Please."

"No, it's just hard to talk about. It feels strange. See, I never told anybody. It's all jumbled." She hesitated again.

"I'm listening," I said.

"Okay. You asked for it. The adventures of Kelsey Lawrence, girl coke-head . . . It happened last December, a couple of weeks before Christmas. I'd gotten this huge coke high right in the middle of the day.

At school. Some of us did coke in the bathroom. Our nice expensive private school, right? My friends and I were doing lines, and they were bragging about where they were going during the winter break. One was going to ski in Gstaad, Switzerland. And Michelle was going to Greece. And so on. And—I don't know—I flipped out. It was the same thing every year, every season. Like I said: a competition. Who has the greatest summer home, or the coolest boyfriend, or the most big-deal parents. And I flipped out. Maybe it was the coke, but I like to think it was me. Something inside me.

"Anyway, I split. I walked right out of the building. I didn't want to go home. I didn't want to go to a movie, or anything. I kept walking and walking, and the more I walked, the more I knew I didn't have anyplace to go. The city felt so unreal. Everybody was walking fast, but *why*? The taxis and cars were all fighting to get ahead of each other. For what? Everybody was rushing to go somewhere, but it was like watching a movie without sound. It didn't make any sense. It was almost funny, but I didn't laugh. I guess I was coming down off the coke, and I felt sad and blank at the same time. How can I describe it? . . . Like my mother, as soon as a handbag gets stained or scratched, she throws it out. She offers it to Nans or Caitlin first, but they have a thousand handbags already. So when the handbag is in the garbage, it isn't a handbag anymore. It's just pieces of leather and cloth stitched together. An empty thing. See, that's what I felt coming off the coke. Like an empty thing. Not a person. A thing. A used handbag. A very expensive used handbag. So I decided to throw myself out. I walked out into the middle of Lexington Avenue with all the cars rushing to nowhere, and I stepped in front of a van."

"Oh, Kelly . . ."

"Not to worry; I'm here. Some guy grabbed me back. A total stranger. I remember, he asked, 'Can't you even say thanks?' And I spat at him, just like that guy in that cardboard box did to me. Because I didn't want him to help me. I didn't want anybody to help me. I wanted to die." Her face looked like a fist again, tensely fighting tears.

"Do you still feel like that?"

"No . . . Sometimes, a little."

"Don't you try it! Please!"

"You're the only person I've ever told."

"Can't you talk to your folks at *all*?"

"My folks? Oh, sure, between the dinner engagements, the parties, the sailing in Newport, the tennis season, the opera season, the charity-ball season, and Wall Street, which is for all seasons. Anyway, I didn't tell them. Maybe I should have." She studied the kids again, deep in thought.

"Are you okay?" I asked.

"Where was I? . . . Oh, yes. I spat at this guy. Don't think I'm proud of that. And I kept walking all afternoon. It was weird. I couldn't stop walking. My mind was down and blank and empty. A real coke down. It's all mixed up. I only remember bits and fragments.

"But I felt after a while—I know this sounds very Hollywood—I felt maybe this was a little miracle for me, that stranger pulling me back. Maybe it was a second chance. And little by little, the real world started coming back. My feet were actually hitting the ground. And I realized how much I'd been out of it. It was as if I were seeing things for the first time. Corny, right?"

"No. I've felt that sometimes."

"And I really started looking around. I must have walked way downtown, and now I was walking back up. I was in the low Forties, I think, maybe not that far from the Starlight. There was some wet snow falling, and the stores had these tacky Christmas decorations, and everything looked so down. One of those porn shops had Christmas lights in the window, right there with the porn magazines and cassettes. And the kids and adults on the street were, like, gray. Gray. Garbage everywhere. And no happiness. None.

"I saw how absolutely miserable some people's lives were. I'd seen all this before, but mostly from a cab. But it was right in my face now. I walked all the way back uptown, up the West Side, past where you live, into Harlem, and it was even worse. Much worse. And I suddenly realized that we were all total shits. Me. My parents. My friends. Their parents. But especially me. . . .

"Do you know, one dress my parents got me for a school dance—and I wanted it!—cost almost a thousand dollars? I once spent over two hundred dollars in one week, on cab fares alone, going uptown and downtown to be at this party and that disco and that swinging restaurant. Don't ask me how much I spent on coke and hash and blue margaritas and God-knows-what. Maybe you were you, Anthony, a year ago, but believe me, I wasn't *me*. I was this druggie bitch . . ."

"What would you have thought of me, if you'd met me back then?" I asked.

"Oh, good question! I would have thought you were a nerdy, dorky, gag-me geek. A total absolute zero. A nothing."

"Oh. What—what do you feel now?"

"Now? Come on, Anthony. You know what I feel. I think I love you more than anyone else in the world. I do. I really do."

It was my turn to fight back a sudden push of tears.

"Are you okay?" she asked.

"It's nothing. Keep going. You were saying?"

"Okay, let me get it all over and done with. It was right then that I decided to become someone else. Right there in the south part of Harlem. There was this little kid, not much older than my brother, Andrew, and he was playing with a bicycle wheel. It was bent. He was rolling it along in the wet snow, and I asked him where the rest of the bike was. He said that his mother was getting him a bike for Christmas, only she was sick, so he was going to build a bike out of all these parts he'd found on an empty lot. And I gave him everything I had, about a hundred dollars, and told him to buy a bike right now. He said he couldn't take it, because they'd say he stole it. So I said I'd go home with him and I'd give the money to his mother. And I did. You saw some of the rooms at the Starlight Hotel? Well, this building was worse. There were holes in the wall and no hot water. Nothing. It was very bad.

"Anyway, I gave the money to his mother. I guess she thought I was nuts, but she took it. And when she asked my name, I said Kelly. Kelly Callahan. I didn't have to think. It just came out. . . . That day. It was *the* day of my life. That day was the beginning of Kelly. December fifteenth, last year. That's the day I was born."

"We should celebrate it every year," I said. "Like a second birthday."

"Oh, that's—that's so nice. Anthony. You're the other best day of my life. The day we met."

"We could celebrate that, too."

"If we keep this up, every day will be a holiday," said Kelly.

"Well, every day we're together *is* a holiday," I said. Kelly smiled at that, her wide Kelly smile. After all that heavy talk, it felt like the sun coming out, to see her smile.

14

WE SAT IN THE PARK for a long time, watching the children play with their toy cars and trucks. We picked out our favorite and watched her maneuver a car along the path. Every so often she fell, *kerplop*, on her rear. It was all I could do to not rush over and lift her up.

"Like I said, I want a lot of kids, Anthony."

"So do I."

"Wouldn't it be weird if we really lasted and did the whole bit: got married and had kids of our own?"

"Just like normal people," I said.

"Normal? What's *that*?" asked Kelly. "Okay! Hey! Let's celebrate being together, right here, right now. Every day's a holiday, right?"

"Right. Want to try some music?"

"Sure. We're not far from the Seaport. How about

another gig there?"

"Great. Better than the subway, any day."

"Unless you get seasick, Anthony sweets."

The South Street Seaport was bustling, as ever. Our favorite spot was free, near the bandstand out on the pier, and we moved in on it fast. I took Kelly's second guitar and played a few warm-up riffs. The tone was glorious. It was another Guild, even better than the one those barf bags had stolen. But just as we began, the Seaport police chased us. We went all the way back out to Water Street and started playing again. This time, there was no problem.

And we had a slaphappy singing afternoon, which we both needed. Our act was great; we'd really perfected it, dancing and all. We did it for three hours with hardly a break. Kelly seemed to be her old self again, full of energy, belting out the songs one after another. The only thing was, I could tell now that some of it—that endless bubbling—was partly a big front. Maybe it is with everybody. Maybe everybody has a story like Kelly's inside them, locked up or kept under a blanket so they don't have to look at it too much. With me it's my father. And my mother. When they fell apart, something in me fell apart, too.

I began to wonder whether I should go down to Mom's opening that night. She'd left it up in the air, almost negative, but I knew I could help her in one way at least: applaud like hell at the end.

During one of our breaks, I asked Kelly if she'd like to see Martine do her opening-night thing. "Hey, great!" she said. "I'd love it."

"I'm pretty sure I can get us in free, if there's seats."

"You don't have to. We can use my plastic."

"No! Kelly, listen. There's something I've got to ask you. Don't be Miss Millionaire's Daughter with me. Please."

"Okay. That's easy. Because I'm not. Not anymore."

But in the flicker of that moment, I thought maybe she was just kidding herself. Maybe I'd caught a glimpse of something. She still lived in that huge place. Caitlin, the maid, was right there to help her with everything. She took cabs without batting an eye. Maybe she'd managed to quit her coke habit, but could she really quit her own life? She was doing all kinds of good things, true, but mostly with her parents' credit card. Maybe there was more Kelsey in Kelly than she thought.

We sang for another hour, then decided to fold our tent. It was close to five thirty. After some crazy eating at the Seaport, going from booth to booth for Greek, Japanese, and Italian fast food, we headed toward the Village and the Griffin Theatre, where the one and only Martine Milano was to do her thing in a few hours.

We strolled in the East Village, soaking up the scene with all the beads and bangles and purple hair, and looking at all the performance places. Kelly stopped at a bistro, The Lost Sheep, that had tables outside and a long bar inside, with more tables. On the window was a poster announcing all the shows for the month of August. Next to it was a flier announcing an open mike at the bistro.

"Hey, how about that," said Kelly. "I've been looking for a place with an open-mike evening. Let's enter it."

"We're not good enough," I said. "Not for this."

"Sure we are! It's an open mike! Anybody can sign on. You said it last: You gotta have faith, Tony-Anthony. It's for next Monday, which is their off-night, but so what? They're going to have a panel of judges."

"It's for near pros."

"We could try. Come on. It's not as if it's the Village Vanguard or some big-deal place like that."

We went inside, and Kelly asked the bartender how to apply. He pointed to the back room. We knocked. After a moment, an elderly man opened the door. He looked as if he couldn't possibly be into our kind of music

"Hi," said Kelly. "How do we enter your open—"

"Simple," he answered, "See that sheet of paper? Can you write?"

"Uh-huh."

"So sign your names."

"Is—is there a fee?" I asked.

"Not here," he said. "Other places, maybe. Here everybody gets their chance. You kids look like you've never done this before."

"We haven't," said Kelly. "Do we have to try out or anything?"

"You want to try out? You can try out. Be my guest. If you're terrible, I'll tell you. Better now than being hurt later. You can play on our stage out front."

"Any special kind of music?" I asked.

"Anything. You can play Beethoven's Fifth Symphony; I don't care. Don't bother with the mike there, because nothing's hooked up right now."

We quickly got into playing position and launched into "Scarborough Fair" because we did it so well together. I played; Kelly sang. She was in top form, I thought. The man sat there, watching every move we made. We did our long version, which took about five minutes. When we'd finished, the man just sat there, though some of the customers applauded.

"Okay. Come to the back room. I never give opinions in the front room."

We were both scared. Was he going to cross us off the list now?

"What's your names? I can't read this entry list without my glasses."

"I'm, uh, Kelly Callahan. And he's Anthony Milano."

"I'm Irv Siegler. You don't have to worry. You kids are good. That's good guitar. A little shaky in the clarity. In the sharpness. You have to play cleaner. But good. Not great. Good. Solid. You could build on that. But you need serious lessons. Find someone.

The talent's there. And the feeling. Ever take lessons?"

"No."

"You've got to put a lot into it. Or you won't get a lot out of it. Find someone good. You! Kelly? Your voice is very good. Very. Trained?"

"Sort of."

"It can hurt you, too much training. For this. Do you do jazz?"

"Yes."

"Rock?"

"Some."

"You have the voice. But there's the personality. I can't answer for that. There's the sexiness. And the acting out. It's an act. You need acting lessons. Absolute must. And you need a hook. A gimmick. Some personal quirk. Something different. But most of all, you need the luck of the Irish. So Callahan, you got a head start, right? Listen to me, you kids. It's a tough, tough racket. I love it. But look at me. All I could do is *this*, finally. I used to play the saxophone. Five other instruments. For thirty years. You ever hear of Irv Siegler? No. Never. But! I bought this bar. I give others a stage. I give all you young people a chance, once a month. And I'm surrounded by music. Friends all over. Why? Because in fifty-five years in this business, I never screwed anybody. And I always tell it like it is, but I also say: Never quit. If you love music like I do, then you'll find a place. A bar, like this. A publicity house. A record shop. Notice I don't say

Madison Square Garden. I don't say Capitol Records. Because I never raise false hopes. Never.

"Your voice, Kelly Callahan, is as good, maybe better, than half a dozen top artists. So what? There's a hundred Kelly Callahans. It's like lightning. Who can tell where it'll strike? I'll tell you something you already know. Half the top people can't sing. You can. So what? The music business isn't music. It's luck. It's pizzazz. It's promotion. It's dog-eat-dog and cat-eat-canary. Notice, I said I love *music,* not the music business. That's my speech. You just took a college course. You're nice kids. See you at the open mike. Stay off the booze. Stay off the drugs. Love yourself, no matter what. Yourself, just as you are. Never mind Madison Square Garden. Seventy-two years of wisdom. You got it free. Good-by and God bless."

"Th-thanks," I said.

"For what? Why shouldn't I set you straight? You'll hear enough bullshit—pardon my French—in this business for the rest of your lives."

We were both a little shaken as we walked back out to the reality of the street. I was only good. Kelly was *very* good. But it was okay; I wasn't jealous. He was right; she *was* very good. And it *was* a tough business.

"So what do you think?" I asked Kelly.

"I think he's saying it like it is. I was thinking of taking some acting lessons on the West Coast. Anyhow, we should feel good, because he thought we could both make it, maybe. So will you do the open mike next Monday?"

"Sure."

"See, wimpo! You didn't even want to try. It's the music business, right? You've got to push your way in."

We continued heading west toward the theater. As we bopped along like a thousand other Village couples, looking beautifully grungy in our ripped jeans and frayed T-shirts, we were tempted to browse in a record shop. But there wasn't enough time to do the high-powered heavy browsing that I get into. I do not leave record shops easily.

And there, coming toward us, unmistakably, was Kelly's friendly enemy or enemy-friend, that girl she'd avoided in Central Park, Michelle. There was a guy with her, and both of them were dressed in the latest all-black super-expensive Japanese designer clothing. There was no avoiding them; we were on a collision course.

Kelly could have stared straight ahead, I guess, but she seemed to have decided on the peace-pipe special.

"Hi, Michelle," Kelly said weakly. We all stopped dead.

"Oh. Hello," said Michelle. It was cool, but not really hostile.

"This is Anthony. Anthony, Michelle," said Kelly.

"Hi," said Michelle, "Uh—Jonathan, Kelsey, Kelsey, Jonathan." I winced when I heard her say *Kelsey*, but what else would she call her? "I met Jonathan in Southampton on the July Fourth weekend." Michelle was actually being pleasant.

"Oh. Good. Great," said Kelly. "It's nice—nice to see you, Michelle."

"Well it's nice to see your face for a change, instead of your back, Kelsey," said Michelle, referring, I guess, to Kelly's retreat in the park last week.

"Ouch," said Kelly in mock pain.

"Speaking of faces, what happened to your face?"

"Oh, a door walked into me."

Michelle seemed to like that. She and Jonathan both laughed. "Good," she said. "So look. The gang will all be back in a few weeks. Meredith's supposed to be back from France right after Labor Day. Speaking phony French all over the place, right? And Jeremy's getting back from Newport end of next week. I spoke to him on the phone. Say, how come you're not in Newport?"

"They're in England," said Kelly. "And I'm doing voice lessons, and so on, all summer. They think."

"Oh. Stuck like me, right? Anyway, look. We're all getting together at the Green Tiger—whoever is back—on September ninth. So come on down."

Kelly shrugged. "All is forgiven, Kelsey. Come home. Is that it?"

"I'm *trying*, Kelsey. I really am."

"I know. . . . Well, hell, who knows! Maybe we will. Anthony can meet the Monster Brigade. He should."

"It'll be, like, the usual time," said Michelle. "Nine thirty, ten."

"Maybe, maybe not," Kelly mumbled.

"I'm trying, Kelsey!"

"I know. I know. Thanks, Michelle."

"By the way, Jeremy says he's got the greatest stuff he's ever seen. There's this dealer in Newport and—"

"I'm off it, Michelle! I'm off it!"

"Okay, okay. The ninth. Green Tiger." Then she winked at Kelly. "Bring him. He's real cute. Ciao!"

I know I must have blushed, because Michelle obviously meant me. But what had happened to her *Go to hell in a leaky canoe*?

"Well, that was intense," said Kelly. "My God, I haven't spoken to her for months. We always used to come down here to the Village. We would spend whole days here and over on Broadway, hunting for trash, with-it, glitz clothes, for the discos and all. No more."

"She didn't seem that angry."

"No, she's giving me another chance. Our rat pack always had one thing: Once the summer is over, forgive and forget. Like everybody's gone all summer, so it's a clean slate again. No grudges. Kind of nice, in a way. So do you want to go, on the ninth?"

"I don't know. Maybe it's good to have peace with your friends. But it's your ball game, not mine."

"You know, one good snort of Jeremy's powder, and I could be gone again. It's like being an alcoholic. I'm going to be fighting it the rest of my life. That's what they told me at the treatment center. I had to go to these sessions for three months. Anyway, don't worry. I'm not going to touch the stuff."

"Damn right! I won't let you!"

"That's good. Well, maybe we'll go, if I'm still here. *If*!"

"Kelly, we've got to move it now. I'm sorry, but my mother goes on in about fifteen minutes."

We sped along Bleecker Street and turned north to Sheridan Square. By the time we'd reached the Griffin Theatre, it was five to eight. I'd hoped to see a mob at the box office inside the tiny lobby, but there were only two other couples going in. I used my Blue Cross card to convince the manager that I was Martine Milano's son. He let us in free with a stern command that Kelly had to put her guitar in the cloakroom.

The theater was only half full. But it was a Tuesday evening and there was no reason to expect a weekend crowd. Except for *Variety*, the only paper that had noticed Martine was the *Times*. It was a small box saying that Martine Milano, a popular actress in Off-Broadway and Broadway roles, was assuming the role of Mrs. X in *The Stronger*. Well, *popular* wasn't bad. But it wasn't enough to generate a sudden crowd.

I saw three of Martine's friends in the audience; her loyal but very shrunken group. I can remember, years ago, when there would be a hundred or more of Mom and Dad's friends and acquaintances in the theater on opening night. I was glad I'd decided to come down; we'd added a few friendly bodies.

I went over to Mom's friends and introduced Kelly. "Kelly, this is Beverly, and Florence, and Lynn.

Mom's buddies." Mom wants me to call them by their first names, too.

"Hi, everybody!" said Kelly in her chipper, upbeat way.

"Oh, *you're* Anthony's friend," said Florence. Mom had told her, of course. "Well, it's nice to meet you. Martine is going to be absolutely great! I did her horoscope, and it is full of good omens."

"Wonderful," I said. Florence is Mom's best friend. She does radio and TV commercials, and can do more funny and weird voices than anyone I know. She used to read stories to me when I was a kid; she was every character, and the trees and ocean as well.

"Can you whistle, Anthony?" she asked. "If you can, whistle like hell at the end."

As we went to our seats, I spotted Mom's agent, Krassman, on the other side of the theater, smoking a cigarette illegally. And I was as tense as hell, despite Florence's prediction. In the old days, I never worried about Mom onstage; she was always in such total control. Or maybe I was too young to understand what a tightrope a performer has to walk every evening. But I was tense. A few late arrivals came in, then a few more, and it helped fill some of the gaps. From Mom's viewpoint, the theater wouldn't look quite so empty now.

The house lights dimmed, the stage lights came up, and we were on our way. In *The Stronger*, a woman, Mrs. X, meets a friend, Amelia, at a cafe by accident, or maybe purposely. And she goes on and on, talking about Amelia's breakup with a fiancé, and about their theater rivalry—the women are both actresses—and about Mrs. X's own family and husband. Only Mrs. X speaks; Amelia is silent throughout.

It develops that Amelia once had an affair with Mrs. X's husband. Mrs. X starts to realize this as she pieces together clues from the past, piece by piece, like a detective. But in the end, Mrs. X tells Amelia that the affair had actually made her own marriage stronger in the long run, while Amelia is left out in the cold. Only it's not really certain who is the stronger one, finally.

Martine was terrific. Terrific. She seemed to dance through the part, sitting, standing, hovering over Amelia, sipping hot chocolate, sending out little barbs one moment, being devastated at the realization of the affair the next moment. Twisting the words, turning them, like the super-wonderful actress that she is. I studied the audience. They weren't moving a muscle; they were hypnotized. Kelly squeezed my hand again and again to signal to me how great she thought my mother was.

Beautiful. Beautiful. It was the Martine of old. The actress playing Amelia was okay, I thought, but Mom was brilliant. She sailed on with lines I knew from the kitchen and living room.

"Everything," she said to the silent Amelia, "even what we did when we made love—everything comes from you. . . . Your soul crept into mine like a worm into an apple, bored its way in, and burrowed until there was nothing left but the skin and some black crumbs. I wanted to get away from you, only I couldn't. . . ."

Her voice rose, fell, was menacing, then playful, sarcastic, angry, forceful. She hit the last line, "Now I'm going home to love him," and strode off with a toss of her head, then a sudden pause, a deep final breath of determined resignation, and the house lights came up.

The audience was on their feet, applauding; they were giving her a standing ovation. It was Mom's best moment in years. She came back on with the actress who did Amelia, and they both took bows, then off, and more applause and whistling, including Kelly and me, and Mom was back, alone, blowing kisses at the audience while the manager took some flowers up to her.

Oh please, please let there be some critics in the audience for this, I thought. But they don't usually review replacements for Off-Broadway shows, and certainly not for one-act openers. Still, it was a million dollars' worth of medicine for Mom. She'd done it. She'd hit a home run.

We worked our way back to the dressing room, a tiny cubbyhole where seven or eight people could create a mob scene. Krassman was there, and Mom's friends, and us. Martine was amazed to see me.

"You came! My Anthony! And Kelly. Did you like it?"

"You were unbelievable, Mrs. Milano!"

"Who in hell is Mrs. Milano?"

"I mean Martine. You were so great!"

"Thank you. Anthony? You haven't said a word."

"Do I have to? You were what I said you'd be: sensational."

"I must admit . . . I *do* think I was good."

There was a general cheer from all of us, and in came the manager looking like an unhappy walrus. "Hey, listen. Keep it down," he said, "Please, we have an audience out there. It's five minutes to *Miss Julie* . . . You were lovely, Martine. Congratulations. Don't quote me, but we should have had you in the first place."

"Thank you," said Martine. "Next time, remember that."

Mom didn't have to stay for the other play, so we left by the side exit, and after Kelly recovered her guitar, we adjourned to a terrific Italian restaurant on Cornelia Street. Kelly and I had our second dinner in three hours, but it didn't stop us. Best of all, Krassman picked up the tab for everyone.

As we left the restaurant, Mom steered me and Kelly toward Eighth Avenue to catch an uptown bus. She still had her opening night flowers. Kelly whispered to me as we walked, "'Tony-Anthony, let's treat your mother to a cab home. Nobody should have to take a bus on opening night. I'll split it with you."

"I guess it would be kind of nice. But let me pay for it."

"No. It's got to be fifty-fifty. Please."

I hailed a cab, and when Martine objected, Kelly told her it was our opening-night present. Mom kept protesting, even as we all piled in. But she loved it, I know, the attention, the flowers, the praise, the works. It wasn't exactly a Broadway opening with limos and flashbulbs. But it was something.

Well, she'd earned it. It was the first time I'd seen her really happy in years.

15

MOM AND I HAD ONE FINAL victory splurge when we got upstairs: huge scoops of chocolate-fudge ice cream with chocolate syrup. Glorious glop! Exhausted but happy, Mom went to her room, flopped on the bed, and fell asleep fully clothed. I put a blanket over her and shut her door. I wasn't tired, so I sat on my bed and tried "Scarborough Fair" again on my guitar, wondering how to play it cleaner as Irv Siegler had suggested. It sounded pretty damn good to me, but I admit, it's hard to tell about your own playing.

Maybe it *was* time to think about serious lessons. I decided right then to get in touch with Luis Alfonso, who I'd seen play in concert. He gives lessons on the side, and considering how terrific he is, they're dirt cheap. I almost started with him a year ago. To hell with saving for the fancy Gibson or Martin guitar. I needed this more.

The phone rang while I was fooling with the guitar. I thought it might be Dad again, calling to congratulate Mom after her opening. But it was Kelly. She'd taken a cab across town to get home. Why hadn't she gone to bed?

"Anthony, did I wake you?"

"No. What's up?"

"I've got problems. I just found out. Caitlin got the call this afternoon. My folks are going to be home tomorrow. Tomorrow! It was supposed to be two weeks from now. There's some kind of emergency at my father's Wall Street investment house. It's, like, *boom,* here they are! I don't know what to do!"

"Don't do anything. Just be normal."

"I didn't take any voice lessons all summer! I wanted to be gone when they got here! I'm not ready for this! Thank God that credit-card statement hasn't come yet. It's got four thousand dollars on it already. I don't know what to do!"

"Kelly, take it easy! Just be Kelsey for a week or so, right? Let them think what they want. You're losing all your cool."

"You're right. You're right. I'm obsessing. I'm reacting like I did when I was six. I was so scared of them then. Here I am, ready to split, and I'm practically hyperventilating because I have to face them. Okay. I'm getting back into focus."

"Can I help you tomorrow?"

"I don't see how. In fact, I may not be able to see you for a day or two. Believe it or not, they expect me to meet them at Kennedy Airport. Caitlin went crazy today. She had to get Alex back from *his* vacation. He's our chauffeur. And Alex had to get the Lincoln washed, cleaned, polished, and everything. See, he was using it for himself. If Dad ever checked the mileage, Alex would be fired."

"So when will I see you?"

"I don't know. Let me call you, if I can, tomorrow. Or if I can't, the latest would be Thursday. . . . Okay. Okay. I've got to get organized. I've got to think. I'm so confused. Am I sounding nuts?"

"A little."

"If you come over, you'll have to call me Kelsey. Can you?"

"Sure. But—do you want me to come over there when your folks are back?"

"I don't know. I'm thinking. Like you keep saying, maybe we can figure something out. I'm trying to find a way. A way that I could stay, and still be *me*."

"Oh, man! That would be tremendous!"

"Okay. But don't get too excited. One of us being crazy is enough. See, I figure, maybe, *maybe* I'll just tell them the whole bit, like it is. About you, about my singing, about the Starlight and the cardboard-box people, and the whole works. Let them *do* something. Let them throw me out. It won't be worse than leaving, right?"

"Great! That's what I was trying to ask you to do."

"I know. . . . I'm thinking. I'm thinking. I don't want to go to San Francisco without you. I want to try to hang in. But I'm afraid of them. They can put you on a pin and make you feel like a bug."

"You mean me?"

"You. And me. Both. They have their way. But it's worth a try. Anthony, I've made up my mind. I'm going to give it a shot. That's it. I'm going to try to be Kelsey again. The *new* Kelsey. I'm going to tell them about you. I am. No fooling around. And about the open mike, and our street gigs, and the works. That's it. It's time for the revolution!"

"Great!"

"Okay. . . . I love you, Tony-Anthony."

"I love you, Kelly-Kelsey."

"It's us against the world."

"And we're going to win," I said.

"I hope you're right."

"I'm always right."

"Good night, Anthony. Wish us luck."

"Good night, Kelly. I wish us luck."

"Good night."

"Good night."

"Good night, again."

"I shall say good night till it be morrow," I said. Mom did Juliet, too.

"It *is* morrow. Good night."

16

I HUNG AROUND THE HOUSE all the next day, but Kelly didn't call. I jumped even when I heard the neighbor's phone ringing through the wall. Martine was bustling around in her manic state, cleaning the place for the first time in weeks. I was so anxious and she was so up that we got on each other's nerves.

"Why aren't you going out, Anthony?" she asked, dust mop in hand. "You're never home in the middle of the day. Do not squander your youth indoors."

"I'm waiting for a phone call."

"Oh. From Kclly?"

"Yes. What's wrong with that?"

"Nothing. It's perfectly wonderful. But you look so tense. Like a horse at the starting gate."

"I am tense. This is a very important call."

"Oh. I will not ask about what."

"Good."

"What?"

"It's too complicated to explain."

"Oh! You mean a dumb actress like me wouldn't comprehend?"

"Okay, I'll tell you. I guess you *should* know. There's a couple of things. First, it happens that Kelly's parents are rich. Like very, *very* rich. And they're getting back unexpectedly from England today. And they don't know anything about me. Or about our street singing. Or anything. Okay?"

"So why be tense? They'll love you. Who couldn't love my Anthony? To know you is to love you."

"Martine, if you're going to give me that kind of bullshit, there's no use talking."

"It's not bull— Your foul language, Anthony, is getting worse every day. You do not hear that from me."

"Except in rehearsals. Anyway, the second thing is, Kelly's thinking of splitting. Because she can't stand them. She's thinking of going to the West Coast; she has a girl friend there who did the same thing. And— and the third thing. I don't know what I'll do if she goes. I don't know. . . . She asked me to go with her."

"Oh . . ." Martine sat down, looking kind of lost. The manic state was gone.

"Just *oh*?"

"And you might go?"

"I don't know."

"Your father's on the West Coast."

"I know! Good grief!"

"So it could be very nice for you. Of course, you *are* still in school and aren't even sixteen and would be throwing away everything, your college education, your—"

"Mom—Martine! I'm not going anywhere."

"You really like her that much?"

"Yes."

"Yes . . ." She said that half wistfully, nodding repeatedly, as if recalling her own past. She was getting very stagy now, very actressy, and I didn't like it.

Why was I so angry! She was doing a poor-me, that's why. Immediately, right away, my problem had to center on her.

"You know, Martine, I have a right to my own life." It just popped out, but I was glad I'd said it.

"I never said you didn't. You're entitled to like someone. To love someone. But . . ." Her face had a familiar sag now.

"But?"

"Well . . ." She was in tears. Real tears, not stage. "I . . . I mean if you left . . . I guess I couldn't stop you . . . If you left—I'd miss you. I'd miss you, Anthony. I'd miss . . ."

"I know. I'd miss you, too. Come on, I'm not going anywhere. Not really. That's why this call's important. She's trying to, like, see if she can hack it with them."

"Can I do anything?"

"No."

"She could live here."

"What?"

"She could move in with us. If it's legal."

"You're kidding!"

"No. Why not?"

"That's an idea! I think she'd want to get out of New York, but it's an idea . . . Except it wouldn't work. She'd never be able to go out in the street. But—Martine. *Mom!* Thank you."

"For what?"

"For that."

"I'd do a lot more than that for you, Anthony."

"I know."

She suddenly took an exaggerated acting pose. "Sir, forgive me, since my becomings kill me when they do not eye well to you. Your honor calls you hence; therefore be deaf to my unpitied folly, and all the gods go with you." More Cleopatra.

"Martine, give me a break."

"You ought to listen. Because I just told you to do whatever you have to do. And go wherever you have to go. That's what love is all about. It applies to both of us. See, Anthony!"

"Thank you."

"And smooth success be strew'd before your feet."

"Please! No more Shakespeare. Why doesn't that phone ring!"

"It will. It's like a watched pot that never boils. Try to get your mind off it. Do something. Work on a song."

"Maybe that's an idea."

I shut myself in my room and tried to concentrate on music. Useless. I was too uptight to do anything but pluck random, nervous chords. It's strange how that happens; last week I wrote my Kelly song in an hour or so. Now, nothing. Not a single phrase or idea.

I went to the kitchen for some supplies, interrupting Mom again. When I'm tense, I get hungry for junk food and leftovers. I'm like a goat; I can eat anything: the grosser, the better.

The phone rang, at last, and I almost dropped my cold hamburger. But it was Jason. I sighed and said hello without much enthusiasm. Jason didn't sound any better. It seemed that the movie was being delayed; it was to be shot in late fall now. And the scene on the pier was being cut. As a result, I was being cut.

"God, I'm sorry, Anthony."

"No problem. I didn't think I had it, anyway." I really didn't care. Too bad, though. Mom would have loved it for me. Or for her.

"That's how it is in the business," said Jason.

"Don't I know it."

"How'd your mother do at her opening last night?"

"Great! She was really terrific."

"Good. She's always terrific. I feel guilty; I should have come down."

"No problem. You missed a great Italian meal, though. A freebie."

"Hey, I gotta go. Nicole awaits. How's things with Kelly? We've got to get together soon, the four of us."

"Things are complicated right now. I'll know more in a few days."

"Anything I can do?"

"No."

"Well, so long, monkey mouth."

"So long, Wainwrong."

It was back to my room for more waiting and still more waiting. Finally, I couldn't stand it. I decided to phone Kelly. What harm could it do? I could be anyone. I dialed Kelly's unlisted number and waited.

A woman answered. It sounded like Caitlin, with her Welsh accent. "Hello. Lawrence residence."

"Uh—could I speak to Kell—Kelsey, please?"

"I'm sorry, she isn't in."

"Oh. Do you know, uh, when she'll be back?"

"She didn't leave word. Who may I say is calling?"

"Oh. Um, a friend! I'll try again later. Th-thank you. Good-by."

I hung up quickly. I didn't want to leave my name; it might mess things up for Kelly. So it was back to waiting. I thought about organizing my records better, maybe alphabetically by group, but I flopped on my bed instead and studied all the familiar dirt marks on the ceiling. I ought to put a poster or two up there.

I waited through the evening, pushing the clock along, until Martine had to leave for the theater. When she left, I circled the phone, wondering if I should try again. I decided not to. Kelly would have figured out who *a friend* was. If she couldn't call me, then she couldn't.

I watched TV fitfully, raided the refrigerator twice, and decided to take a shower. I was certain the phone would ring if I was in the shower. It didn't.

I slept badly that night. I guess I have a hyper personality; I awoke a dozen times. Sometimes I thought I'd heard the phone ringing. But obviously Kelly wouldn't call me at four in the morning.

I slept till ten. Still no phone call. There was a note from Mom on the kitchen table. She'd gone out with Florence to shop for new drapes for our living room. Good. We needed them, and it was good and healthy for her. At the end of the note she'd written: *Did your call come? I hope it was good news.*

Again, I wondered if I should call Kelly. This was slow torture. Why couldn't she call? Were her parents tapping the line? I sat around, listless, trying to force the clock to speed up. I read the papers; I studied the street below from the window; I thought about another shower. And the phone rang. I leaped to it.

"Hello!"

"Hi. It's me. Anthony, I'm sorry I couldn't get free yesterday. Can you hear me? I'm talking low."

"Yes."

"I haven't had the guts to tell them yet. It's, like, there's so much going on, now that they're back. It's a real zoo. I've got to play their game for a day or so. I've got to find the right moment."

"I understand."

"You can't believe how my mother's tied me up with things to do. But I told her I'm seeing a friend on Saturday, so that's okay. So listen, can we meet at one on Saturday? How about in the lobby of the Whitney Museum? That's, you know, at Madison and Seventy-fifth."

"You mean I can't see you till *then*! This is only Thursday."

"I can't help it. Can you hear me?"

"Yes! Yes!"

"To make it work, I figured this is the best way, playing along for a few days. I'm being Miss Dutiful Daughter. So when the revolution comes, they won't blow me over. Okay?"

"I guess."

"I think my mother's suddenly trying to notice me, after sixteen years. It was my swollen cheek. I told her I got mugged, and she's suddenly the good mother. I should have said I walked into a lamppost. We're going shopping today. Gasp!"

"Good. You'll meet *my* mother buying drapes."

"So I'll see you Saturday, at one? At the Whitney?"

"Right. Will we be doing a gig? We could try some songs for the open mike. That way we can practice and make some money at the same time. How's that for efficient?"

"Great! But maybe bring *your* guitar this time, Tony-Anthony. I don't want them to ask a million questions about why I need a guitar to go out with a friend."

"Okay. No problem."

"Okay. So long, Tony-Anthony, sweets. I miss you."

"I miss you, too. So long, K.K.K."

"K.K.K.? That doesn't sound too great."

"That's Kelly-Kelsey-Kook."

"Oh. You are so right."

17

I BROWSED THROUGH THE ART BOOKS at the sales counter in the huge lobby of the Whitney Museum. The place was mobbed with tourists; you could hear people speaking Japanese, French, German, Spanish, Italian, and even Russian. The artists in the books were the same as the artists in Kelly's apartment: Franz Kline, Roy Lichtenstein, Georgia O'Keeffe, on and on. And again I wondered what a nothing like me was doing hanging out with a super-rich girl like Kelly.

As I browsed, I heard a high-pitched nasalized voice in my ear. "I am sorry! You are under arrest for putting your filthy fingerprints on our clean books!" I turned and did a double take.

It was Kelly, but a totally new and different Kelly. I couldn't believe the transformation. She was dressed in a yellow-and-pink flowered dress with earrings and bracelets and this and that. Even to my inexpert eyes, it was all very designer-original and stylish. Even her shoes were drop-dead expensive. She was wearing light makeup; the bruise on her cheek was barely detectable under the expert touch.

"Hi, Tony-Anthony."

"God!"

"Surprised? It's the only way I could escape without an FBI investigation. Just call me Kelsey Super-Prep, and you'll be fine."

"You look—unreal."

"I feel unreal. I'm so used to being total Kelly for these last five or six weeks."

"Why didn't you let me know? I'm dressed like a jerk. I've got my worst jeans on."

"I couldn't get free to phone you. I couldn't help it, Anthony. My mother was all over me."

"You actually look . . . *nice*."

"It's bad. I'm beginning to relapse. I really like being dressed great for a change. People notice you. Isn't it sad?"

"I don't know. Is it?"

"It is. It is. My brain could be blank as a balloon, but so what? It isn't what you are, it's what you wear. And so, Tony-Anthony, you may accompany me this awftanoon, dahling, if you simply walk five steps behind, thank you veddy much."

"Should I go home and change?"

"No! Please. Stay the way you are and help me

keep sane . . . Hey, Anthony. There's someone I'd like you to meet. Would you be willing to go with me to the sailboat pond in the park before we do our gig?"

"Sure. But how can we do a gig if you're dressed like that?"

"Oh, we'll be great. People love to see weird couples. It makes them wonder. You watch and see how many people stare at us when we walk. Come on. I want you to meet—this person."

"Who? Not your mother!"

"No, no. You'll see."

We walked across to the park, and she was right. People looked at us, turned, then looked again. Who was that geeky guy in torn jeans and a Rolling Stones T-shirt, with that elegant, wealthy society girl in that gorgeous dress? Maybe her bodyguard? Or her wayward brother just home from jail?

"This is weird," I said. "I've never been stared at like this before."

"You think this is something? You should have seen me in the old days, with my crowd in our disco rags. It was Halloween every night. See, that can be a drug, too. Dressing up."

We were at our old haunt, the sailboat pond. Kelly strolled along the edge of the pond, then stopped and pointed toward two boys of about seven, working on a remote-controlled sailboat at the water's edge. The boat was taller than the boys. A second boat, not quite as large, lay on its side on the pavement.

"See those kids over there?" she said. "The one on

the right is Andrew. My brother. The other kid's his friend Brian. And over there, on that bench—see her, that lady in blue?—that's Nans. My Nans. I'd like you to meet them."

"But I'm dressed like a nerd."

"Don't worry. They're on our team."

Nans—or I should say, Mrs. Callahan—looked just like her photo: She had a round, warm, friendly face. Still, I was tense as we walked to the bench.

"Hi, Nans," said Kelly. "This is Anthony, who I told you about? Anthony, my one and only Nans."

"Hi, uh, Mrs. Callahan," I stammered.

"If you're my Kelsey's friend, then I'm Nans to you, too," she said. "How do you do?"

"Uh, Kell—Kelsey's talked a lot about you. Nice to meet you."

"And the same," she said. "I see you like playing the guitar, just like Kelsey, don't you?" She pointed to my guitar.

"Oh. Yes. I—yes!"

"Well, a love of music is a fine thing to have. You know, do you not, how well Kelsey sings?"

"Yes, and she screams pretty good, too," I said, thinking of our mugging in the park. I was trying to be funny, but it seemed awkward the moment I'd said it.

"Ah, and I can vouch for that," said Mrs. Callahan. "She was all lungs as a baby, you know. I suppose all singers are. Oh, what a racket it was."

"Nans, it was not!"

"I ought to know. I was there."

"So was I," said Kelly.

"But I have witnesses. Your mom and pop."

"You mean they actually were around to *hear*?" said Kelly.

"Ah now, hush, hush. They love you in their way. They do. Besides—" Mrs. Callahan looked at me, as if the family beans were being spilled.

"Oh, Anthony knows how I feel. But let's not get heavy. . . . How's the Pain behaving?" She gestured toward Andrew.

"That boat is too much for him, it is. He's having trouble. The sail sticks in place. Do you know something about machinery, Anthony?"

"I could try," I said. "Should I?"

"Sure," said Kelly. "If you fix it, you'll be his hero forever."

We went over, and Kelly did the introductions again. Andrew didn't even bother to look up. "Hi," he said. "I can't get the sail to go left. I think it's broke." Direct and simple, as if he'd known me all his life.

We pulled the boat out of the water, and I studied the mainsail and the guy lines that led to the motor. I saw right away what was wrong. There was a kink in the line that released the sail to the left—was that starboard?—and it wouldn't slide through a metal loop. Kelly, Brian, and Andrew watched as the Amazing Milano undid the kink and hefted the boat back into the pond.

"Try it now," said Captain Anthony. Andrew fiddled with the remote box, the sailboat caught a breeze, and it was on its way. Fixed.

"Yow!" Andrew shouted. "Thanks! Now we can race, Brian!"

For the next hour, Andrew and I raced his boat, the *Dragon Queen*, against *Super Eagle*, Brian's boat, while Kelly and Nans sat and talked as if they hadn't seen each other for months, which they hadn't. When I finally called it quits and went back to their bench, Nans said, "Now that's what I call a nice young man. To play with children is a lovely thing." But I'd never had a remote-controlled sailboat. Never. For that hour, I hadn't been a nice young man at all; I'd been a seven-year-old myself. A kid among kids.

"Okay," said Kelly. "We've got to go, Nans. We have things to do. We'll see you tonight."

"Do be on time," said Nans. "You know how they are."

"I will. I will."

We said our good-bys and took off. But I'd caught something there. *We'll* see you tonight. I asked Kelly what she'd meant.

"Oh. Yes. Right. I didn't want you to get all uptight about it. I was going to tell you after we finished our gig. Well . . . they know about you now. I told them last night. And they'd like to meet you."

"Meet me? So soon? They just got back?"

"See, you're not from our crowd. You have to be inspected like imported meat. You were supposed to come over for dessert, which is crazy, but that's them. I changed it to dinner. May as well go for the works, right?"

"But—I'm not ready for that!"

"I know. But this way we can get it over with. I want to know where I stand with them. Who I *am* with them."

"But what about me? Look how I'm dressed."

"You could go home and change, but I wish you wouldn't. I want them to meet you exactly as you are."

"I'll look like a jerk! You're stacking the deck against me! Against us! It's not fair. You could have told me on the phone. You're doing this for yourself! You want me to look bad, so they'll make fun of me, and you can say to hell with it and go to the West Coast! Is that it?"

We walked through the park in silence. Kelly was thinking in that kind of inner-struggle way she had, as if a battle were going on.

"Maybe you're right," she said finally. "I don't know. I guess I want to test them. I want them to like you, the way Nans does. She likes you, you know. Can you tell? You're the only guy I've gone out with that she's liked. . . . Okay, I'm sorry. I'm wrong. I guess you should get dressed and all. I'm sorry. I think it's just my anger at them coming through. We should do our best, not our worst."

"Hell, yes!"

"You know, it's good, Anthony. You always give in

too much, with me. I like to see you take a stand sometimes."

"Okay! I did!"

"You should do it more."

"Okay! I will!"

"Good. I mean it. It's good."

We walked for another minute, then Kelly stopped, led me off the path and under a tree, and looked up at me.

"Please. Can we make up?"

"I was never un-made up," I said, but I kissed her anyway, and we hugged silently for a long time. I knew she was right about my giving in too much. To her. To my mother. To everyone. Even to Jason. She was right. But maybe I'd never had anything really worth fighting for, before. Now I did. And now I would.

18

WE DID A COUPLE OF SETS down by the zoo, but I wasn't really with it. My mind was on the dinner, and my crummy clothes, and the underarm deodorant I needed to buy, and the table manners I'd never learned.

"Have some dinner ahead of time," Kelly warned me. "If you eat as if you're hungry, they'll notice it. The best thing is to leave something at every course. That's probably why I pig out when I'm away from home."

We split at four thirty, and I zipped home to prepare for the big scene. Martine had left for the theater early, thank goodness, so I was able to go crazy by myself. I raided the refrigerator three times, because I was nervous and because of what Kelly had said.

The magic hour at the Lawrences' was seven. I showered, checked every inch of my face, cleaned and trimmed by fingernails, and even changed my socks because there were holes in both heels. You never could tell; they might have X-ray vision.

I took me over an hour to get the right combination of slacks and shirt and shoes. I almost went out to buy a new shirt but finally settled for a light-blue one that made me look like an off-duty cop. When I hit the street, I decided to shoot the works and bought a small bouquet of wildflowers for them. It seemed like the right thing to do.

At six thirty, with the slightly droopy flowers in hand, I got a cab and went across town, feeling so tense I was afraid it would show. The cab got to Kelly's building within ten minutes. I walked into the park and sat, trying not to think. I felt cold sweat under my arm and down my chest. I wished I could go home for another shower.

At exactly 7:01, I walked into the lobby. It was a different doorman.

"Uh, Anthony Milano for Kelsey Lawrence." Should I have said *the Lawrences*? I wasn't sure. When it comes to etiquette, I am a total idiot.

"Thank you," the doorman said politely. He called the apartment and murmured something into the phone, and I was on my way to the elevator. I tried to work some saliva into my mouth, but it was as dry as a desert.

Kelly was right at the door, ready to intercept me.

She was still in her pink-and-yellow dress. "Wow, Anthony! You look gorgeous! Are those flowers for me?"

"For, I guess, your mother."

"Good touch. But make them for, like, everybody. Keep it vague. Come on in. They won't bite. I hope." She seemed pretty tense herself.

We went into the huge living room, with all the sofas. Kelly's mother was there. She looked a little like Kelly, but her face was wider. She was short and slim and dressed very mod; her skirt was unbelievably short. Next to her, Kelly's dress looked super-conservative.

"Well, hello there, Anthony. I'm Diana. So nice to meet you." She had a beautiful English accent, but her voice seemed strained, as if it didn't quite belong to her. She was pleasant enough, though.

"Hell—hello. Nice to meet you," I said, trying to be confident.

"Oh, what lovely flowers."

"For, uh, you know, you people, uh—"

"Why, thank you. We'll have Caitlin put these in a vase and place them on the dinner table. Wouldn't that be nice. Caitlin!"

Caitlin appeared out of nowhere. She seemed to know exactly what to do about the flowers with hardly a word spoken. "Do call Mr. Lawrence," Kelly's mother said to Caitlin.

"Yes, ma'am."

"Well, now. Kelsey's told us a little about you, but she didn't tell us how tall and tan you are." I felt a light twinge there. The *tan* did it. I don't know why, but it bothered me. Maybe it was the combination, as if my being tan were as permanent as being tall. Was she trying to say how Italian I looked? Or was she just being friendly? I couldn't catch Kelly's eye for any hint. *A mick donkey*. Kelly had warned me.

"Oh, I'm not that tan," I said, my heart banging away.

"Well, but it's so healthy-looking. We've been in England—did Kelsey tell you?—and you know England. Not nearly as much sun as here, not even summers."

Kelly's father came in. He was as slim as Diana, but tall and graying and very dignified-looking. He was dressed in an old sweater, scruffy brown corduroy slacks, and jogging shoes. All right!

"Oh, you would wear *that*," said Mrs. Lawrence softly.

"My evening to relax," he said. "Time off." He gave me a big smile and held out his hand. "Hi, there. I'm Kelsey's pop. Robert to you. How are you, Anthony?" They certainly knew my name. That was something.

"Hello. I'm f-fine. How are you?"

"Busy. Terrible, getting called back from the first long vacation I've had in years, two weeks early. But that's business. Would you like a drink? Some white wine? Perrier?"

"Uh, wine would be good." I hoped it would relax me. My mother's excuse.

"Kelsey, how about you?"

"Perrier."

"Diana?"

"Wine would be just lovely. Come on, let's sit down and get to know one another. . . . Those trousers, Robert," she murmured. "And that sweater."

Robert winked at me, as if to tell me he'd done it to provoke her and was sharing it with me. I was beginning to kind of like him. There was something of Kelly in him, I thought.

We all sat down at one of the groupings of sofas, while Robert whispered something to Caitlin about three wines and a Perrier. There was a stiff moment when no one spoke. I noticed Diana tug her skirt down nervously, though it didn't budge. Mom did that sort of thing onstage, purposely, to indicate that the character she was playing wasn't as sophisticated as she seemed. I observe a lot from Mom's stage gestures. And I remembered Kelly saying how her mother was always trying so hard to be what she wasn't. And what she wasn't was a miniskirt wearer. It made me a bit less uptight; she was only human, after all.

"So, Anthony," said Robert finally. "Have you lived in New York all your life?"

"Yes, sir."

"Oh, come on now; no *sirs*. We're all friends here. Any friend of Kelsey's— You can let your hair down and relax."

"Uh, are you from New York?" I asked him. "I mean, did you grow up here?" Not exactly relaxed, but I felt I had to say something.

"Oh, sure. This was my dad's place. But Diana was born in England. And your folks?" He was acting very friendly and warm; they both were. But I was being given the third degree, and I knew it. I decided to let them have the whole works, in one shot.

"My father was born in Brooklyn. And my mother's from Chicago. She's an actress, and he's a director. They're divorced. She's Martine Milano. I doubt if you've heard of her. And he's Sal Milan. You might know of him from movies."

"Sal Milan. I can't say that I have. Have you, Diana?"

"No . . ." she said, looking very thoughtful. "I don't think so. But Martine Milano. The name seems familiar. Shakespeare?"

"Sometimes."

"Oh, I think I *have* heard of her. Well, isn't that interesting. Do you act, Anthony?" She tugged at her skirt again.

"I play the guitar."

"I see. So does Kelsey. Of course, you know she sings."

Caitlin had come back with a tray of drinks and some tiny hors d'oeuvres. She placed everything on a glass-topped coffee table between us.

"I know," I said. "She's great."

"We think so," said Diana. "Naturally, we're the proud parents, so we're a bit biased. Did she tell you she'd been asked to sing with the New York City

Opera this next season? A small part, but still . . . Think of it, at her age. Did she tell you?"

I looked at Kelly. She bit her lip and shrugged apologetically to me. I read her unsaid words as *I'm sorry; that's something else I forgot to tell you.*

"Uh—no," I mumbled.

"She's too modest."

"I'm not modest," said Kelly. "I'm not going to do it, so there was nothing to tell."

"Well, of course you are, dear."

"Of course, I'm not."

"Maybe she's right," Robert said. "It's too soon."

"It will never happen," said Kelly.

"Well," said Diana, "this isn't something to debate in front of Anthony, now is it? This is something we can—"

"Oh, yes it is. Anything you want to say to me can be said in front of Anthony. I mean it."

"I see," said Diana. "Very well. I'll take that to heart." Another skirt tug, an angry one. Her voice was cool, but her gestures were giving her away. Thank you, Mom the actress.

"I've been meaning to tell you both," said Kelly. "It's like—Anthony and I have been singing together in the park. And at the South Street Seaport. Even in subway stations. You know: pop, folk, jazz, rock. That's how we met. I've been doing it all summer, while you were away. I didn't take any lessons. I don't want to do opera. I wanted to tell you in front of Anthony, because he's very—" She was almost in tears.

"He's very important to me. I love singing this kind of music. And that's what I want to do. We're going to perform at an open mike this Monday, down in the East Village, and you can both come down and see us. You can bring all your friends, too. And I hope you'll be proud of us."

"I see," said Diana again. "Mm-hmm."

"Well," said Robert. "Give us a couple of seconds, all right? This is—a surprise."

"You could have guessed, Dad," Kelly said.

"We're not God almighty," said Robert.

"Anyway, that's the way it is."

"I see," said Diana.

"If you say *I see* again, I will scream," said Kelly. Then, with a deep breath, she added, "Sorry. I lost my cool."

I was obviously in the middle of Kelly's revolution. She had saved it for now. I didn't know what to do. I didn't know what to say. I tried to take a sip of wine. It didn't help. I was numb.

"Well, Kelsey, you have the right to do whatever you wish with your life," said Diana incredibly calmly. "If you choose that path, that's your choice. But we don't have to applaud it. If you think at sixteen—you told me to say what I wish in front of your friend; I'm sorry, Anthony—if you think at sixteen this family has to cater to your every whim, you have, indeed, another think coming." All calm as glass. But she kept smoothing her skirt nervously. Mom could learn a few gestures from her.

"It's not a whim. I'm just telling you that I'm a human being, and this is what I want to do with my life. And I wish—I wish you'd support me in it. There's something else. I may as well say it all. I've been using my credit card all summer to buy food for people on welfare. Instead of voice lessons and other junk. Four thousand dollars, so far."

"Four thou— Good Lord!" said Diana, finally losing her cool. "Good Lord!"

"All right, Kelsey," said Robert. "Now you're in *my* territory. Sorry, Anthony. Feel free to leave if you like. That's more than a hint—"

"He stays right here!" said Kelly. But this had nothing to do with me! I felt trapped!

"Fine. That money wasn't yours to give away. It's ours! You have absolutely no right whatsoever to use it for anyone or anything but your summer expenses and lessons!" Her father was *not* calm; his face had turned crimson. He took a huge belt of his wine. He was no longer Mister Buddy.

"Then I broke your wonderful laws. Have me arrested!"

I was feeling like an idiot, sitting there. She should have done this before! And she was being so aggressive. It was bad.

"Stop fuming, Robert," said Diana. "Don't you understand, Kelsey? It's your not asking us first. We give lots to charity. You know that."

"Only when it gets you on the board of the Met or this or that big-deal group!"

"Let me finish. We should have the right to give our money in our own way. We might not choose to feed people directly because it doesn't solve the underlying problems of—"

"I know!" said Kelly. "But the way you do it, it all ends up in someone's computer! That's right, isn't it? Well, I decided to give my voice lessons and French lessons and stupid fall clothes to people who are hungry. Tell me what's so wrong about that?"

"It's not your money to give," said Robert. "That's what!"

"It isn't yours either! It's from buy-out leverages or leveraged buy outs or whatever those things are. It's from deals. From pieces of paper. It floats around like dust. I wanted to do something *real* with it."

"All right," said Diana. "Let's let that go. You certainly meant well—Robert, please! Let's talk about something else. Anthony is here. Let's talk about Anthony. You can't speak without his being present? Fine. Then you both must be very serious about each other. Are you?"

"Yes," said Kelly.

"Anthony?" asked Diana.

"Yes," I said.

"Well. And you two are going to sing in the street for your supper, so to speak? Like flower children? Is that how it's going to be? Street buskers? That's what they were called in England. Glorified beggars. My parents had to fight their way out of poverty, Kelsey, as you well know. And it wasn't much fun, I can tell you. You seem to want to fight your way back *in*! It's hopeless!" For a brief moment, Diana had dropped her guard. There was real pain in her eyes.

"Mom, it's okay. We'll be great," said Kelly, trying to convince her. Kelly had clearly seen the pain. "We make a great team, and we'll play real gigs someday. Somebody who knows heard us play, and he thinks we can make it, if we work at it."

"So you have, as they say, great expectations. Well, I'm tremendously relieved. Someone *told* you. Quite wonderful." Kelly bit her lip at the sarcasm. "You needn't look like that, Kelsey! But tell us, just how long have you two known each other, anyway? Three days?"

"Two weeks."

"Oh, perfect! Does Anthony have any idea how many boys you've known for two weeks?"

"Yes! What are you trying to do?"

"And does he know—since you're so close, and I can say *anything* in front of him—does he know that you've had an abortion?"

"N-no."

"And does he know—"

"What are you trying to *do*! What?" Kelly turned toward her father. "Dad! Please!"

"Just let her finish," he said. "Go ahead, Diana."

"Does he know that you've run away three times in the past two years?"

"No. . . ."

"No? But you're so *close*! And one more thing,

while we're at it. Does he know you were arrested for possession, twice? Does he? That it was all we could do to keep you from being sent to a juvenile detention center?"

"No!"

"Now he knows."

"Yes." Kelly sat there, tears streaming down her face.

"So, Anthony, how do you like your blue-eyed girl now, as Mr. Cummings would say?" Another skirt tug; a victory tug.

There was absolute silence. I took a deep breath and let it all sink in for a second. I decided to keep my cool, no matter what.

"I-I love Kelly just as she is," I said. Kelly gave a slight sob at that, and dropped her head.

"Oh, *do* you! You don't even seem to quite know her name. It's Kelsey, you see."

"I call her Kelly. I know about her problems. She's quit drugs. And she's quit the other stuff, too. And I love her just as she is."

"Of course, she *is* very, very rich, isn't she." Calm as metal. Calm as ice. This was the Diana Kelly was running away from; I could see it so clearly now.

"When I met her, I thought she was poor. I didn't know who she was or where she lived. In fact, I wish she *was* poor. Then everything would be easier."

"Bravo!" said Diana.

"People say 'bravo' in the theater for good acting. I'm not acting. What other things do you want to tell me about Kelly? That she's generous? That she cares about people who are hurting? That she's sick of the way she used to be? See, there's things I can tell you, in case you didn't know. How she's brave in a lot of ways. Braver than me."

Kelly was watching me now. She wasn't crying anymore. She looked as if she'd made up her mind. I knew about what.

"You seem rather brave to me, Mr. Milano," said Diana. It sounded sarcastic.

"No, I'm not. I don't understand your 'bravo.' And your Mr. Cummings. And your suddenly calling me Mr. Milano. It's, like, if I want to tell you something, I say it right out front. I don't hint."

"That's known as being blunt," said Diana.

"Look, Anthony," said Robert, trying to be Mister Buddy again. "This isn't fair to you. You've come into the middle of a family thing. I think you're a nice kid. But we've had a lot of problems, as you can see. A lot of problems. And what Diana is trying to say is that your seeing Kelsey is just adding to the problem."

"Well, it wasn't me who got her into drugs and everything," I said as calmly as I could. "It was her friends, not me."

"I see you're quite an expert on our lives," said Diana. "As if *you* people don't have drugs. And *everything*, as you put it. Can't you tell an unstable person when you see her staring you in the face?"

"What do you mean by *you people*?" I asked.

"Never mind. Do you have anything more to say

Kelsey? If not, I really think this is a very poor evening for having a convivial dinner. That's why I suggested dessert. But perhaps we might leave that for another time, too."

"Come on, Anthony," said Kelly. "Let's go. We've got to talk."

"*We've* got to talk!" said Diana to Kelly.

"Later," said Kelly. "Anthony, let's go. Please."

"Kelsey, I really don't appreciate your charging out of here," said Diana.

But Kelly was up and heading for the door, and I, of course, had to follow. None of us said good-by or anything. It was like my father's angry exits after he and Mom had split up and he'd tried to see me at our apartment.

We were in the elevator and on our way down. Kelly was huddled in a corner, hugging herself protectively as she sometimes did when she was feeling miserable.

"Now you know," she said. "About everything."

"You told me most of it. You just left out some of the gory details, right?"

"Oh, God. I'm not the generous one, Anthony! You are!"

"I'm not that generous. Like, why in hell did you have to do that credit-card scene with me there? After that, nothing went right."

"I guess it was like vomiting. Everything came out. Don't worry, Anthony. They would have strung you up just the same. That's more important to them than the money. Notice my mother let it slip: suggesting only dessert, right? Because she knew this would happen. She knew."

"I guess you're right. . . . You're going to San Francisco, aren't you?"

"You bet!"

"Okay. I'm going with you." I didn't think I'd say it till I said it. "I'm going with you," I repeated.

"You are? Do you mean it?"

"Yes. Yes, I do." I was scared. But I'd said it, and that was that!

"That's so fantastic!"

"I've made up my mind. That's it. I'm going."

"There's one thing my mother said that's, well, something you should think about. Even though she tried to wreck us with all those things. I *am* unstable, Anthony. I'm a mess. I am. Maybe it won't be so great, being together."

"That's okay. I'm good with messes. I've had lots of practice at home."

"God, I love you, you—you tall, *tan* Italian!"

She'd caught Diana's remark, all right. "Smile when you say that, sister," I said. "Where I come from, them there's fighting words, pardner."

19

IT WAS WHAT MY FATHER HAD DONE. As we walked over to a fast-food place on Lexington Avenue, the thought stung me like a small insect buzzing somewhere in my brain. I was going to California with *my* girlfriend. It felt strange, like when I'd first seen the back of my head in a double mirror. The back of my head was the same as my father's. We were like twins. And would my leaving hurt Mom as much? I didn't want to have to think about it. Not yet.

Over burgers and shakes, Kelly told me about her plan. She'd obviously been working on it for months. She'd taken a lot of her own personal money out of her bank account, enough for a Greyhound ticket to the coast and a couple of months' living expenses. The money, she told me, was under her mattress at home. She even had some false ID's she'd gotten in one of those junk stores near Forty-second Street, with her photo, and the name Kelly Callahan, and the address of her friend in San Francisco. Had she done this those other times she'd left? She seemed to be an expert.

"So how soon can you go?" she asked.

"I don't know. Maybe in a few weeks."

"A few weeks! I want to split tomorrow, if I can. There's a bus that leaves at six thirty tomorrow evening. Can you do it?"

Mom had said I should do whatever I needed to do. What were her words? *Your honor calls you hence*. Okay. Maybe fast was best. No time for arguments, or debates, or tears, or scenes from old plays. Mom was flying high now, and I had a life to live. So I wasn't sixteen yet; so what? In the old days, people left home even younger. I wanted to go. I *would* go. I could taste and smell it: this—this freedom ahead. This was the high bar I was going to walk. And not look down or look back. With Kelly. Together. Us.

"Okay," I said. "Tomorrow."

"One thing, Anthony. This one last time, let me pay for your fare—"

"No. I've got money saved."

"Use it on the coast."

"No!"

"Okay, whatever you want. I'm going to leave my place very early tomorrow morning, while they're still asleep. When could we meet?"

"I need some time with my mother. Let me have the day with her."

"Sure. So how about if we meet at five P.M. at the Greyhound ticket office. It's in the main concourse at the Port Authority."

"Okay. . . . You know, it's too bad. We're going to miss that open mike."

"No problem, Anthony. We'll just have to wait till we're in San Francisco to amaze the world. I've got one real problem though: I have to travel light. I can't take much stuff. I hate to leave all my records and tapes. My friend out there, Alison? She was able to ship her stuff, but there's no way I can."

"I think I can get my mother to send my junk out there. Can I give her your friend's address?"

"I wish you wouldn't. My parents know your mother's name now, and they might try to find me through her. They're very thorough. They love it, playing detective."

"Maybe she could ship it to General Delivery, San Francisco."

"Hey, that's a good idea."

We talked about ways of covering our tracks. Kelly even suggested wearing some sort of disguises for the bus. I felt like I was in a James Bond movie. And I must admit, the whole thing did seem kind of crazy.

And I was feeling weird. Kelly seemed so calm about it all, as if she were taking a trip to the beach for the day. As we finished our cheeseburgers, she took out some pictures of San Francisco her friend, Alison, had sent.

"Alison lives in the Mission District, where there's lots of people from Mexico and South America. Look at these kids playing right out in front of her building: There's a black kid and two Mexican kids and one Vietnamese and a kid from Australia, she wrote. She says it's great, like the United Nations. You don't see this sort of thing in New York much, kids all playing together like this. In New York, everybody has their own ghetto."

Kelly showed me some photos of murals painted on the sides of buildings, huge beautiful paintings, and a photo of a mural painted in explosive colors on the walls of a narrow alley to make it look bigger and brighter. These murals were typical in the Mission. And in all the photos, there were kids playing and people sitting in front of their buildings. It did look very warm and friendly.

"If you like Mexican food," Kelly went on, "wait until you try it there. Alison says it's sensational and very cheap. And the Mission is only one area; there's so many mixtures of people and neighborhoods. San Francisco is the greatest city in the U.S., I think. We can do our gigs down in Ghirardelli Square, and Golden Gate Park, and downtown, on and on. Alison says it's perfect for that. And no winters, Anthony."

"Will I be able to stay with you at your friend's place?"

"Yes! It goes without saying! She's great! You'll like her. . . . You don't look all that convinced. You're not quitting on me, are you?"

"No. I'm going."

Kelly was bubbling on about how she would pack during the night, and leave early by the old reliable service entrance, and pick up our tickets to make sure we had them. She seemed so eager to go, while I felt all sorts of battles happening inside my head and guts. What was I doing?

We dumped our food trays and went out into a light drizzle. I like how the city looks in the rain. We strolled aimlessly, not saying much, but not wanting to go home. Not yet. Maybe we were both giving New York a silent farewell. We stopped for coffee and Danish, then walked some more. It was wild. In less than twenty-four hours, I'd be on a bus to San Francisco.

20

I GOT HOME VERY LATE. It was still drizzling; my shoes were completely soaked. I hoped Mom had gone to sleep; I didn't feel like talking about San Francisco that night. It would be better after Sunday breakfast.

But something was wrong. The front door was unlocked. Mom never left the door unlocked. I checked out the kitchen. There were smashed dishes everywhere; thousands of fragments covered the linoleum like the pieces of a jigsaw puzzle.

We'd been burglarized, was my first thought. I rushed to the living room. The TV set was on, but Mom wasn't there. A dish must have been thrown against the far wall; the shards were all over the rug, as if a fragmentation bomb had exploded.

Then I smelled the sweet sour smell of wine. Oh,

no! Oh, no! Her bedroom door was shut. I knocked. No answer. I went in. The lights were out, but I could hear a low moan in a corner of the room. Mom was sitting on the floor, leaning against the bed, an empty glass in her lap and a bottle of Chablis beside her. The room smelled of wine and vomit.

"Go 'way! Go 'way!"

"It's me! Mom—Martine, it's me! Anthony!"

"Anthony? . . . Give me my robe! Put on my crown! I have—I have—immortal longings in me! Now . . ."

"Mom. What happened?"

"Now no more—the juice of Egypt's grape—shall moist this lip. That's a laugh, you bastards! Yare, yare, good Iris, quick. You bastards! You bastards! I hear Antony call: I see him—rouse himself to—to—praise my noble act. You bastards!"

"Please, Mom! Tell me! What happened?"

"They closed the show . . . Six performances. Closed. The end. Good-by . . ."

"You'll get other parts. You'll have other plays."

"Oh, yes. Oh, yes. Ah ha ha ha ha ha."

"You will."

"Twinkle, twinkle—little star . . . little star . . . that's me. . . ."

"Let me help you get into bed."

"Go 'way! I don't want to ever see you again, Salvatore! Do you hear me, Salvatore! Get out! *Get out!*"

"It's me. Anthony."

"You bastard! Salvatore! You—you—"

"Anthony. It's Anthony. Salvatore's gone. He's gone.

He's in Los Angeles. Please, Mom."

"In Los Angeles. With his whore!"

"Mom. Please. Let me—let me help you into bed. It's Anthony. Anthony . . ."

"Anthony?"

"Yes. Yes."

"Get me some more wine. The bottle's empty."

"No!"

"How dare you—cross your mother."

"When you're like this, you're not my mother. You're a two-year-old!"

"My oblivion is—is a very Antony. Is a very . . ."

"Get into bed!"

"No. I—prefer the floor. Where I belong. With the rest—of the garbage. Ah ha ha ha ha ha ha!"

I pulled the pillows and blanket from the bed and tried to get her comfortable. I propped a pillow behind her back, and the other under her head. Then I covered her with the blanket. She didn't resist. She seemed to be falling asleep. This was bad, but tomorrow would be worse, I knew. Tomorrow would be the crash.

I decided to clean up later. I had to call Kelly. I couldn't go with her. I couldn't. Not with Mom like this. No way. I didn't want her to buy a ticket for me. I had to call.

I dialed her unlisted number. Everything seemed unreal. Who would answer? Caitlin? Kelly's mother? I heard the ring. Once. Twice.

"Hello?" A woman's voice? A girl's?

"Can I speak to— Kelly, is that you?"

"Yes. Anthony? What's up?"

"My mother. She's dead drunk. They closed the show. She's the worst I've ever seen. Kelly, I can't go. I just can't."

"Okay. I understand."

"I'm sorry. I'm sorry."

"So am I. . . . I knew it would fall through. I knew it."

"If I go, I don't know what would happen to her. This isn't a one-day thing with her. I'm sorry."

"I'm still going, Anthony. I've got to."

"I know."

"Tomorrow? Can you still meet me at five? At the terminal?"

"Y-yes."

"Please come. Please?"

"I will. I'll be there."

"And bring some photos of you. Could you?"

"Yes. And you, the same."

"Anthony, if it makes you feel any better—if you went with me, with your mother like this, you wouldn't be the Tony-Anthony I love."

"Thank you. . . ."

"Hey. Nothing is forever. I'll get back. Or you'll come out. Or we'll meet halfway."

"Right. Right."

"Tomorrow at five? The Greyhound ticket office?"

"I'll be there."

"Good night, Tony-Anthony. Don't worry. It

wouldn't have worked out anyway. I'm too crazy."

"No, you're not!"

"Just try living with me for a month. See you tomorrow."

"It would have worked!"

"If you say so. So long."

"So long."

I sat there and stared at the phone for a long time. Martine had done it again! But this time she was going to a doctor, even if I literally had to drag her. And a shrink, if she needed one. And Alcoholics Anonymous. The works. I wasn't going to be sucked into the self-defeat quicksand she wallowed in half the time. And neither was she! No more! No more!

I was going to take control of things. I was! Maybe last December fifteenth was Kelly's new birthday. Well, today was mine!

21

THE PORT AUTHORITY BUS TERMINAL was pretty empty that Sunday afternoon, except for the street people seated or lying at the edges of the huge main concourse. The Greyhound ticket office was an open area right off the main plaza. Kelly was there, standing to one side, wearing her torn jeans and moccasins and red headband. She was loaded down with her backpack and guitar and a huge duffel bag. She walked toward me, dragging the duffel bag along the floor.

This time, *I* was late. It was after five thirty, but I hadn't wanted to leave Mom until Florence had gotten to our apartment.

"Hi. I'm sorry," I said. "I couldn't get away until—"

"That's okay. How's your mother?"

"Not too good. She stayed in bed all day. I called

her friend Florence, and she's there right now. We're going to get her to a doctor tomorrow. That's the first step."

"Good luck. I know how lousy your mother must feel. I've been there . . ."

"Do you know, a few days ago, when I told her how you couldn't stand living at home, she offered for you to live with us. You still can."

"No. It's really, really sweet of her. But no."

"Think about it. It could work."

"No. I can't stay in New York. I tried something like that, once. With a friend. But they found me. When you can, thank your mother for me. . . ."

We went over to a brightly lit fast-food place on the other side of the wide concourse and ordered soda, chicken salad, and bran muffins. We sat down at one of the tables, surrounded by Kelly's duffel bag, guitar, and backpack, and ate in a kind of sad silence. Then we exchanged photos. There was one of Kelly on a huge sailboat, more like a yacht, and another on a horse, and a couple of shots in front of an enormous country house. She was giving all this up.

"Is this your house in Newport?"

"That's it. . . . It feels funny, doesn't it? Waiting for the bus? Like waiting to be executed."

"I brought you some sandwiches for the trip."

"You didn't."

"Here." I handed her a small paper bag.

"Oh, that's so nice. We stop to eat, you know."

"I know."

"Well, there's something I have for you. This is yours." She took her guitar, which was leaning against the table, and slid it over to me.

"No! I have a guitar!"

"It's dumb to take this all the way to California. It'll probably get wrecked on the bus. Alison has a good guitar out there, and she says she never uses it. Please. I want you to have it. It's like a dying wish. You have to take it. Please?"

"Okay. I'll hold it for you till you come back. Or I get out there."

"Good." She handed me an index card. "Here. It's my address and phone number at Alison's. We'll talk on the phone, and we'll write. Okay? Don't look so down."

"Right . . ."

"It takes about four days. I'll call you as soon as I get there. Or maybe even on the way, if I can. But the thing I want to say, Anthony, is the next time I see you, I want to be with you all night and all day. And I mean all night. I wish it could've been now. But things have been so messed up."

"I wish it could be now, too. I wish it could be always."

"It will. It will. Don't look so down. Please."

I was suddenly feeling the reality of her going. I started swallowing hard, again and again. The world was blurring.

"Don't look so down," she said again. "Let me go. If you're down, maybe I won't be able to make it.

Please, Anthony. Let it happen. Please?"

"Okay . . . okay. . . . I'll tell you what my mother told me. It's a line from Shakespeare: Your honor calls you hence; therefore be deaf to my unpitied folly, and all the gods go with you. I mean it. I do."

"Thank you, Anthony. That's worth more than a thousand guitars. Thank you."

We walked downstairs to the Greyhound platform area, and held each other while the bus pulled in. We held each other while people got on and the luggage was put into the huge storage compartment. We didn't say a word; we just hugged and hugged so that the hug would last a long, long time.

Finally, Kelly pulled away from me and walked past the ticket guy onto the platform beyond a steel and glass partition. I couldn't follow without a ticket, so I had to watch her though the glass of the partition. She gave them her duffel bag and walked to the open bus door.

At her bus window, she tried to smile. It was hard to see her now. I tried to smile back. Then the bus closed its door and slid out backward from the platform and rolled toward the other end of the terminal, toward the Lincoln Tunnel and New Jersey and Pennsylvania and Ohio, and on and on. I stood there with her guitar while everything blurred, stood there alone, but at the same time moved with her, westward, like a cell that splits, like a double image.

I don't know if I'll ever see her again. I don't know if she'll stay there, or come back, or disappear into the real world that can hurt people like my mother, who aren't toughened for battle. But I know that whatever happens, for a little while she and I had the real thing. The real thing.

And wherever she is, wherever she goes, I know that I'll love her forever.